The Ten Point Woman

by

Hava Mendelle

ISBN: 978-1-7643534-3-4 (Paperback)
ISBN: 978-1-7642228-1-5 (eBook)

Published by Lived Press

The Author

Hava Mendelle has always wanted to write love stories. The Ten Point Woman is her debut novel — a quirky rom-com she imagined like a good meal: not too complicated, not too heavy, yet moreish and satisfying. She lives in Australia with her wife, two children, and more half-finished to-do lists than she cares to admit.

Chapter One

The perfect wife will…

1. Be Jewish (it's my heritage)
2. Be 170 - 175cm tall (optimum kissing height)
3. Have long, dark, curly hair (but I don't mind blondes)
4. Be good-looking (i.e. hazel eyes and freckles)
5. Be between 30 and 35 years old (older, more serious)
6. Have a good career (ambitious)
7. Have a stable family (no drama)
8. Want to get married
9. Want children

"That's only nine points," Leo says, adjusting his glasses. "You said it was a ten-point list."

"Eh, nine's enough." Satisfied, I cap my pen and set it on the kitchen table. Leo pulls the notepad closer, somehow managing to flex his biceps in the process. His bald head gleams under the fluorescent lights. My cousin looks like a pro-wrestler who wears glasses as part of his disguise as a financial planner.

Now he's shaking his head. "Bracha, we need numbers. Figures. I can't work out probabilities with this. Where are the stats?"

"I don't want to overcomplicate this," I reply, snatching the notepad back. "All I need is a list that's short and specific. Like me."

"Lies."

"I am short."

"But you aren't specific."

"What do you call this?" I wave the list at him.

Leo rolls his eyes. "Schoolgirl bullshit?" I flip him off and he swats my hand. "Mind if I turn on the fan?" he asks.

"Sure."

It's almost eleven on a Monday night and the air is already thick with summer humidity. I can see beads of sweat popping on Leo's forehead as he leans back in his chair to flick the switch. We're in Mum's kitchen, the place where all great lists and plans are made, and I've brewed a whole pot of coffee despite the fact that Leo doesn't drink the stuff for reasons I can't understand. Through the open window, I can just make out a brushtail possum scrambling up the back garden fence. He doesn't care that mating season is over. He's on the prowl.

That's the attitude I need. It's never too late, right? Even though Mum's gone.

I squeeze my coffee mug, pretending to study the list. But once again, my mind is replaying that conversation with Mum about how she hoped I'd settle down with a nice girl, that she'd see me happy with someone nice, that I wouldn't be alone if she were gone. I looked around at mum's things, she was my best friend (which is actually an understatement). She never judged me or my dating life. Not that I felt judged, exactly, when she'd held my hand and smiled and started talking about my future wife. More surprised, since I'd never indicated any interest in marriage. Not to her.

Not to anyone, really.

Not even to Leo, who moved in with me and Mum when he was twelve and is like a brother. Much more so than my actual brother.

"Okay, I'm just going to say it," Leo says, snapping me from my thoughts. "What about Maddy?"

I laugh. "Maddy doesn't want serious."

"You've asked her?"

"Don't have to." I take a sip of coffee. "She's poly."

"Hate to break it to you, but polyamorous isn't an antonym of serious."

"Not the point." I tap the notepad. "Besides, Maddy fits maybe two out of nine. Max three."

"She's a great cook," Leo points out. "Why isn't that on your list?"

"I'm not marrying a woman for her cooking."

"I sure could."

"Yeah, well. You're a man."

"Yet you hold the one-night stand record." Leo arches an eyebrow. "Maddy's one of the few repeat visitors. I'm just saying, maybe there's a reason for that."

"What, like I'm madly in love with Maddy and I don't know it?" I laugh. "Give me some credit. I'm not that stupid. Besides, I'm not looking for romance. I'm looking for a wife."

Leo lets out a half-laugh, half-groan. "Bracha…"

"What?"

He's silent for a moment, fixing me with that

analytical gaze he usually saves for complex financial statements. "I'm just wondering if maybe this isn't the best time for making big life decisions. I don't think you are thinking this through."

"What do you mean?" I ask even though I know exactly what he means.

"I know you want to move on, but maybe you should slow down on this."

I bristle. "Shiva ended ages ago."

"Ah, right, I forgot that a week is *ages* in Bracha time."

"It's why I'm aging so fast," I deadpan, pointing to the wrinkles between my brows.

Leo chuckles. "You still look eighteen. Act like it, too."

"I'll take that as a compliment." I glance up as the light overhead flickers. I changed the bulb a few days ago but the wiring in this place is ancient. When I look back, Leo's wearing his Concerned Cousin face and I sigh. "Look, this has nothing to do with Mum, okay? I'm just…ready for a commitment and a life-long plan."

The words roll awkwardly off my tongue like I've got a mouth full of marbles. Leo stares at me sceptically but I hold his gaze. Then he lets out a sigh and grabs my notepad.

"Okay," he says, pulling a pen from his shirt pocket. "We've got a clear image of your future wife. Now we need to figure out the stats on where you're most likely to find her."

***

Dad calls the next morning, three minutes before my alarm is set to go off.

I grab for the phone buzzing on my nightstand. "Hello?"

"Bracha? Did I wake you?"

"No," I lie, sitting up and running a hand over my cropped hair. "What's wrong?"

"Nothing!" Dad sounds mildly offended. "Does something have to be wrong? Can't I just call my daughter because I want to talk to her?"

I make a face, fighting the urge to say, *You can, but you don't.* Mum was the "call just to chat" parent. The dreamer. Dad's the practical one, like me. We only ever talk out of necessity. It's why we get on so well.

"Sure you can," I say, standing and heading to the closet. "But I'm leaving for work soon, so I can't…be…long." The last two words are stretched over a loud yawn.

"Late night?" Dad asks knowingly.

"Mmm."

"Did you have a date?"

I pull the phone away and stare at the screen to confirm I am, in fact, talking to my father. "Nope. No date. Just me and Leo."

Dad never asks about my love life. To Dad, I will always be his little girl and I like that. It's not that I'm keeping my sexuality a secret from him. It's just that we don't talk about my dating life. At all. Ever.

"Ah," Dad says. "How's the house? Did you ever

get someone to come in and look at the bath upstairs? Because I'm happy to do it."

I swallow a sigh and pull a pair of scrubs from the closet. "All taken care of," I say. It's not exactly a lie. Calling a plumber is on my list of things to do. My parents bought this house in the '90s, a bright white modern coastal two-story that was gorgeous back then. Still is, but now it takes a lot of upkeep. Mum always kept on top of it, at least until the last year or so of her life.

There's a long pause. I wiggle into my scrubs, struggling to keep my patience. Dad's hesitation is practically radiating from my phone and I wish he'd just get to the point. It's not like him to beat around the bush.

"Remember our old apartment?" he says finally.

I freeze with one arm shoved through my shirt. "In Israel?"

"Yeah." Dad pauses. "We all thought it was so small back then. But it was kind of nice, wasn't it? The kitchen, especially. I loved watching your mother cook in that kitchen."

I don't know what's going on with him but I don't like it. His voice is thick with grief, with guilt, with other emotions I don't want to examine.

"Yeah, she was a great cook," I say shortly. "Look, Dad, I've got to get ready for work, so—"

"Eli's getting out on parole."

I almost drop my phone.

"What?" My heart slams against my ribcage. My brother was sentenced to a year in prison six months ago on drug charges. It should've been longer. A life sentence, if it were up to me. Isn't that typical for voluntary manslaughter?

Okay, fine. I know no judge would actually convict him for causing Mum's death. But Eli's selfish behaviour, his terrible choices—they're the reason she spiralled into depression. He's the reason she's gone. As far as I'm concerned, he deserves to be locked up indefinitely.

Dad's still talking, but it's hard to hear over the buzzing in my ears.

"…good behaviour. I spoke to him yesterday and he, ah…he'd like to talk to you about the inheritance."

My skin goes cold and clammy. My chest is rising and falling heavily and I realise my breaths are coming in bursts.

I squeeze the phone hard. "There's nothing to discuss," I say shortly. "It's a fifty-fifty split and I'm the executor of the will. I know he's pissed about that but it's what Mum wanted."

That's downplaying it. Eli must absolutely loathe that Mum gave me that kind of control. Well, I loathe that Eli gets half of everything. It's not about the money. I don't need it. It's that Eli doesn't deserve *anything*. He'd waste it all, just like he's wasted every other opportunity he's ever had.

"He isn't contesting that," Dad replies. I can hear the hesitation in his voice and it only fuels my anger. "He wants to talk to you about the house. About…options."

Options? My mouth is open, but the words are

lodged in my throat. I live here. Leo lives here. It's been our home since we were kids. What could Eli possibly want with it? No way he wants to live with us—he was barely here as a teenager and he moved out the second he was of legal age. He can't have any nostalgia about this house. He barely shows any interest in our family. He has no loyalty to us. This place doesn't mean anything to him.

Then, a far worse thought hits me.

Does he want to *sell*? Is that why Dad brought up the plumbing issues?

Rage and fear grip me by the throat.

"I've got to go to work," I manage to choke out. "Bye."

I can hear Dad talking as I end the call. My hands are shaking. I stand there, staring at my reflection in the mirror, left arm in the sleeve with the rest of my shirt bunched up on my shoulder. My hair in a mess. I look about as unstable as I feel.

"Fucking Eliyahu," I mutter, shoving my right arm in the sleeve and yanking my shirt down. Then I shove my feet into my shoes and head downstairs. My brother might think he has "options" when it comes to this house but hey, it wouldn't be the first time he was completely wrong.

Chapter Two

The nurse—Kia, I think her name is—looks up the moment I enter cubicle two. I'm stationed in the Adult Acute Unit today, which is nice; I needed a faster pace to keep my mind from drifting.

"This is Henry Roberts, presenting due to complaints of chest pain," she tells me briskly. "He's got a bit of a—"

"That's fine, thanks," I interrupt and Kia falls silent as I turn my attention to the elderly man sitting up in the bed. His eyes are glued to an iPad on his bedside table where some sort of trivia competition is playing out on the screen. I glance down at his file which tells me he is seventy-six and was diagnosed with Alzheimer's nearly three years ago. Nil cardiac history.

Henry lifts a shaking arm and points at the screen. "See now, if I won that kind of cash, I'd buy a caravan. Always wanted to live on the road, you know? Have a real adventure."

There's a poorly placed IV cannula in his right arm that is wiggling as he jabs his finger at the screen to emphasise his point.

Kia hovers nervously. "Mr. Roberts, you should—"

"Hi, Mr. Roberts," I say loudly. "I'm Dr. Cohen. How are you feeling today?"

"Like a million dollars!" A wide, friendly grin

splits his wrinkled face and I can't help but smile back. "Know what I'd buy if I had a million dollars?"

"A caravan?"

His eyes widen with genuine surprise. "That's exactly right! Always wanted to live on the road, you know?" Henry gestures, tugging at the IV on his arm. Kia twitches a little as if she's ready to leap forward.

"Travel keeps you young," I agree, still skimming the chart.

Henry beams. "That's right, that's right. Say, any chance lunch is on the way?"

There's a half-eaten sandwich on his table and an untouched cup of coffee.

"It just arrived." I point to the coffee, then flip to the next page on his chart.

Henry's eyes light up as he surveys the sandwich. "Wonderful," he murmurs. "There's a good lad."

I glance up, eyebrows raised. Henry offers me another warm, open smile, then reaches out to pat my hand. The older the patient, the more likely they are to think I'm a man—a boy rather —never mind the scrubs, the name badge, the earrings, and the fact that I introduced myself as Dr. Cohen with a deep yet feminine voice.

Kia moves forward again. She reaches out, and for a second, it looks like she's going to place her hand on Henry's in a *Go Team!* gesture to save that IV. I press my lips together to hide my amusement.

"What's that?" Henry appears to notice the needle taped to his inner forearm for the first time. "Is that a…in my…"

His papery skin drains of any remaining colour and his eyes slide out of focus.

"Mr. Roberts!" I move forward as the man slumps back against his pillows. Kia tuts her tongue and places the cardiac monitor back on.

"As I was trying to say," she tells me, "He's got a pretty severe needle phobia. Took ages to get it in with four of us nurses."

"Ah." I slide the clipboard into the plastic slot at the end of the bed and pull my stethoscope around my ears. "Can you see if the ECG is available?"

"Of course." Kia hurries off and I don't miss the look of relief on her face.

Henry's heartbeat is strong and in just a few seconds his eyes flutter open.

"Hello again, Mr. Roberts," I say, even louder this time. "Feeling okay?"

His bleary gaze is fixed on the screen. "Like a million dollars," he mumbles. "Know what I'd do with that kind of money?"

"Buy a caravan and go on an adventure?"

Now he looks at me and I see a ghost of a smile. "Exactly. There's a good lad." He tries to sit up and winces. I place my hand on his back, accidentally bumping the IV. Henry glances at the needle fixed to his forearm.

"Is that a…in my…"

I groan as his eyes roll back again. This time, he slumps forward and I catch him by the shoulders just in time to prevent a face plant into the coffee cup. But his head rolls and bumps the egg sandwich, which ends up all over his lap.

"Perfect," I mutter, gently pushing him back so he's resting against the pillows. I snatch a roll of gauze from the emergency tray, keeping an eye on him as I break my personal record in speed bandage-wrapping. His lashes start to flutter just as I press a piece of tape to hold it in place.

"What's this?" He slurs, half-lifting his arm and staring blearily at my work.

"Just a little scratch!" I say cheerily. "Got you all fixed up."

Blinking, Henry smiles at me. "Why, you're a lovely young woman! Are you married, by any chance?"

I return the smile as I clean up the sandwich with a tissue. "Nope. But I'm looking, Mr. Roberts."

Over an hour later, I'm typing up my notes on Mr. Roberts' acid reflux. When I got to work this morning, things were hectic enough to keep me occupied. But now that I've had the chance to slow down, I can't stop glancing at my phone every few seconds.

I'd shot off a short email to my mum's lawyer a few minutes after hanging up on Dad, asking whether I could legally withhold Eli's inheritance because he wasn't of sound mind. I'd attached all the documentation I had containing records of all his petty crimes and his conviction. Eli literally squandered his freedom in exchange for drugs. No way should he be trusted with even a dollar of his inheritance. He'd be using again within a few days.

Mum would be heartbroken, knowing her final gift to him was what sent him back to prison.

"Sounds like you had an exciting morning." Victoria, the nurse manager, leans against my desk and stirs a paper cup of coffee with a plastic straw. Her shiny black hair is swept up and held in place with a clip that somehow manages to look practical and stylish at the same time.

I stare at her blankly, my mind still on Eli. "How did you know?"

"Kia," Victoria says, licking the straw. "Henry's a sweetheart but he's a repeat customer to ED—always forgetting to take his meds."

"Oh." My shoulders relax and I scratch an itch on the back of my neck.

My phone buzzes and I snatch it up, but it's just a text from Leo about picking up a few curries for dinner. With a sigh, I reply *No thanks*, toss my phone down, and stare at my notes. My handwritten words swim before my eyes.

"So, what's going on?"

I glance up at Victoria, who's watching me with a shrewd expression. "What do you mean?" I ask.

"I mean, you're distracted," Victoria says bluntly. "It's not like you. So, what's up?"

"Just…" I lick my lips, trying to gather my thoughts. *It's just that I want to call my dad and scream some sense into him. It's just that my brother has never shown any of us that he has the potential to change. It's just that I don't know what he could possibly want with Mum's house, and the fact that he's even asking scares the shit out of me. It's just that he didn't even go to her funeral—because he was in prison, yes, but that's still his fucking fault.*

"It's just family stuff," I say finally, shrugging as I pick up my pen again. "The usual. You know."

"Hmm." Victoria studies me over the brim of her cup. I struggle to keep my face neutral. Usually, I talk pretty much everything over with her, personal and professional. Victoria is like a hybrid mentor-older sister who has looked after me ever since I was a medical intern here at St Vincent's, and she's quick to call me on my bullshit. But I can't wrap my head around this Eli thing yet.

I can feel her gaze boring into me and I know it's only seconds before she presses further. Which is why I blurt out: "I've decided to find a wife."

Victoria's red lips are a perfect O of surprise. "Find a what now?"

"A wife." I grab my bag from beneath my chair and pull out the list. Victoria takes it, her brows disappearing under her bangs. "Behold, a list of qualifications for those hoping to be Bracha's perfect woman."

"Oh, my," Victoria says, blinking comically as she scans the list. "This is…something. You know anyone who fits these criteria?"

"Not yet," I reply. "But she's out there and I'm going to find her. I've got a plan. Well…I'm working on one." When I look up, Victoria's face is scrunched like she's holding in a laugh. "What?" I demand in what can only be described as a petulant tone.

"What do you mean, *what?*" Victoria shoots back.

When a serial dater with a list of one-night stands longer than my dissertation tells me she's got a plan to get married despite never having a relationship that lasts past breakfast, I assume said serial dater is making a joke." She waves the list. "And an elaborate joke at that."

"It's not a joke." I grab the list and shove it back into my bag. "And you're missing the point. I've been a *serial dater*," I pause, curling my fingers into air quotes, "because I didn't want to get married. Now, I do. The logical way to proceed is to decide exactly what kind of woman I'm looking for so I can find her faster."

"This is so adorably naive," Victoria says with a chuckle. "Bracha, honey, if all we needed to find the perfect partner was to know what kind of person we wanted, I would've been Mrs. Jason Momoa years ago. You can't manifest the perfect wife."

I wrinkle my nose. "Who said anything about *manifesting*? This isn't some woo-woo magic. This is a plan, based in logic."

"Because love is so logical," Victoria says with a snort. "Come on, now. Many things in life are predictable, Bracha, but love isn't one of them. It's messy."

I shake my head. "Love isn't messy. *People* are messy. An organised person can find love in an organised way—a *predictable* way."

When I scratch the back of my neck again, Victoria moves forward and flicks the tag. "Cute look," she says, and I look down, horrified to realise—

after a full five hours at work—that my scrub shirt is inside-out. "Yep, you're not messy at all, honey," Victoria says with a wink.

Glancing around, I pull my top over my head, reverse it, and slide it back on. "I had kind of a rushed morning."

"I'm sure." Victoria's expression softens. "Hey, listen. Whatever this family stuff is…"

I stiffen, keeping my gaze on my shoes.

Victoria pauses a long moment before continuing. "I just want you to know that if you want to take some time off work to relax, to process, to grie—"

"I don't need time off," I interrupt. My pulse is suddenly racing and I can't meet her eyes.

"Okay," Victoria says. "I get that. But if you change your mind, just let me know and I'll speak to the boss."

I nod, turning my attention to filing my notes on Henry Roberts. When I look back, Victoria is gone. Sighing, I slump down in my chair and check my phone. Nothing from the lawyers. Feeling antsy, I open my texts. Beneath Leo's messages are chats with my aunt Agatha, Dad, and Maddy.

My thumbs hover over the screen as Victoria's words echo around my head. Finally, I tap out a quick message.

Hey! Want to meet up tonight?

Maddy's response comes seconds later.

Hell yes.

My entire body relaxes, and I slide my phone into my pocket.

Hey, I do want to find the perfect wife. Really.
But I'm not married yet.

***

I spot Maddy on the dance floor the second I walk into Harper's Bar and I can tell from the particular way she's wiggling her arse that she's at least three drinks in.

She beams when she sees me and I wave before heading to the bar. Cade slides a gin and tonic toward me with a wink before moving on to take other orders.

"Thanks, gorgeous!" I call, then drain half the glass. I'm usually not a big drinker. But nothing's been usual about today. If a needle-phobic Alzheimer's patient and a shrill woman with horrific gas insisting she needed her appendix removed despite multiple tests that said otherwise weren't enough to distract me from Eli, maybe alcohol would do it.

Alcohol and a night with Maddy.

Cade has another gin and tonic at the ready before I set my empty glass on the bar. I sip this one more slowly, watching Maddy grind against another club regular I vaguely recognise. She's cute—same goes for most of the women here tonight—but there's a reason Maddy's attracting glances like she's magnetised. She's gorgeous in the most conventional sense of the word, a tall blonde with bright blue eyes and a ten-thousand-watt smile. We've been friends for the better part of a decade—friends with benefits for almost five years, ever since the night her ex dumped her, and my attempt to comfort her turned into something a little more. In a lot of ways, Maddy and I have the perfect relationship. The sex is great, the friendship is great, and neither of us is interested in anything romantic or exclusive.

Except now I am. I slip a hand into my pocket to feel for the list and smile. Maddy's going to get a kick out of this. "Going all monogamous and boring," she'll say, or something like that. But unlike Victoria, she won't make any assumptions that this has something to do with my grief over Mum. Maddy won't give me sympathetic smiles or eyes filled with pity. She'll give me a hard time, which is her way of being supportive, and that's exactly what I need right now.

I finish off my second drink and leave the glass on the bar. Seconds later, I'm sliding between Maddy and the vaguely familiar cute regular who shimmies off to find another dance partner.

"Hey there, stranger," Maddy says, and I can smell the tequila and lime on her breath. She slides her arms over my shoulders and clasps her hands behind my neck "Thought you'd forgotten I existed."

"Never," I reply, pulling her hips closer to mine. "It's just…you know. Been a rough week."

Maddy nods, her fingers brushing the hair at the nape of my neck, sending an electric current down my back.

"I get it," she says, lips curved in a half-smile. "Bet I can make you feel better tonight."

And this is exactly what makes Maddy the perfect

friend. No pity, no urging to talk about my feelings or take time off to grieve. Just no-strings-attached sex.

I love Maddy, I really do. As a friend.

We spend the next hour on the dance floor, then move to the bar for another round of drinks. I listen as Maddy talks about her heinous day at the bank thanks to some new computer program that keeps glitching, then counter with my own story of Henry and the IV. By the time I finish, she's wiping away tears of laughter.

"Okay, you win," she says. "So, what else is new? How's Leo?"

"He's fine." I pause, my thoughts shifting to Eli. "Actually, he's helping me with a little project."

"Oh yeah?"

"Yeah." I grin at her and lift my glass to my lips. "Finding the perfect wife."

I tip my head back and polish off the gin. When I look back at Maddy, her expression is a mask of confusion. Confusion and some other emotion I can't quite place. Or maybe it's just drunkenness.

"The perfect what?" she says, and that little slur from earlier is gone.

"Wife." I set the empty glass down. "I want to get married."

I wait for the teasing to begin, but her blue eyes sparkle with anticipation—like she's waiting for me to drop the punchline. And to be fair, I can't blame her for thinking this is a joke, so I launch into it.

"Mum told me before she died that she wanted me to find someone." I notice a fleck of lime on

Maddy's chin and brush it off with my thumb. "And I know this is going to sound crazy, but the more I thought about it, the more I realised I want that too."

"Really?"

There's a softness in her tone that's way too intimate. And way too sober.

I lower my hand. "Really. You okay? How many have you had?"

Maddy waves this question off. Her gaze is locked onto mine. "I'm good. I'm great, actually. I…I wasn't expecting this tonight."

Expecting what? I almost say but don't. I feel slightly off-kilter, like I'm missing something important. "Yeah, well, that's my plan," I finish vaguely.

Maddy bites her lip. "So, this future wife of yours…anyone I know?"

I relax a little at her playful tone and pull the list from my pocket. "Maybe. You tell me."

She takes the paper and unfolds it slowly. I can tell she's holding her breath, though I can't imagine why. I glance over at Cade, suddenly in need of another drink but he's busy.

When I look back at Maddy, her smile is gone.

"You don't *mind* blondes?"

I let out a shot of laughter. "Don't take it personally."

But she's not teasing. Any hint of playfulness is gone as she skims the rest of the list.

"Good career…*ambitious*…well, I know you don't think I'm…" she trails off, meeting my gaze.

It's only now, when I see that flash of

disappointment that I finally realise what her eyes had held earlier.

Hope.

"You're fucking kidding me, Bracha." The words are hard, clipped. "You mean to tell me, in all seriousness, that you want to get married to some random hypothetical woman when I'm standing right…."

She stops, closing her eyes.

Thanks to all the gin, the words tumble out of my mouth before I have a chance to think better of them.

"You didn't think I meant you, right?"

I know right away I've made a mistake. Maddy practically growls as she takes a step back, shaking her head in disbelief.

"No, of course not," she spits out, drawing the attention of more than a few drinkers. "Why would I, Bracha? We've only been doing this—" She points back and forth between us, "—*this,* whatever this is, for five years. I mean, sure, I was there for you when you didn't pass your first med exam, I was there for you when your brother went to prison and your mum died. I was there for you every time you wanted to cry, or to laugh, or to fuck. But hey, I don't have…" Maddy shoves the list at me and I let it fall to the ground, too stunned to move. "Brown hair, right? And I'm too tall? Not *optimum kissing height,* although I never heard you complaining."

Half the women on the dance floor are staring at us now. I swallow hard and take a step closer to her, but she pulls away again.

"Maddy, come on," I say half-heartedly leaning over to pick up the list. "It's not…I mean, you don't actually want to get married. Or have kids."

"Oh, because you know what I want?" Maddy snaps. Her eyes are shiny with unshed tears, and guilt cuts through me like a knife. "Here's the crazy thing, Bracha. I actually thought I didn't want those things. But lately I've been thinking maybe I would with the right person. That's how normal people figure it out, you know. They meet someone and realise what they want *with that someone*. They don't just decide they want a wife and make a fucking list." She flicks the paper in my hand and I flinch.

"Look, I didn't——" I press my lips together, hotly aware of all the stares and blatant eavesdropping. "I didn't know you felt that way," I say, lowering my voice. "I mean, come on, Maddy. Weren't you just telling me about finally hooking up with that barista a few weeks ago?"

Maddy throws her hands up. "And? We're not exclusive, are we? Oh, I get it," she says suddenly, snapping her fingers. "You think being poly means I'm anti-marriage. Because apparently you don't know open marriages are a thing. And I know this is going to blow your mind, but couples in open relationships? They have kids sometimes."

"You don't want kids, though." Once again, I mentally curse the gin for loosening my tongue. The truth is, Maddy's never mentioned anything about kids. I just assumed it was a no. Apparently, I made a lot of false assumptions about one of my best friends.

Maddy sweeps a shiny lock of hair from her eyes. "I don't know what I want, Bracha." All the venom is gone from her voice. Now she just sounds tired. "I thought maybe I was figuring it out, but clearly, I had it all wrong."

"Maddy—" I reach for her arm, but she shakes me off.

"Don't." Maddy flicks the paper in my hand again. "Good luck finding a wife, Bracha. There isn't a single woman in Australia who could live up to your ridiculous expectations."

And she turns on her heel and storms out of the club.

I stand and watch her go. Dozens of women are staring at me, but I don't care. I'm too confused to feel embarrassed at the moment. Maddy and I had never talked about getting serious. We were anything *but* serious. How could she have misread our relationship so badly?

I turn back to the bar and signal Cade for another drink.

"You alright?" he asks as he pours, giving me a sympathetic smile.

"Yeah, it'll be fine," I say with a shrug. "Just a misunderstanding."

He hands me the drink and moves further down the bar. I pick up the glass and stare down at the clear liquid. A misunderstanding. Right. That's all. Maddy misunderstood, well, everything. As I drain the glass, I ignore a tiny, nagging voice in the back of my mind.

Did she misunderstand it? Or did I?

***

Two hours and three beers later, I know the answer.

"She was just drunk." There's a slur to my words and somewhere in the fog of my mind, I register the irony. "I bet I get a text from her tomorrow apologising for the whole thing."

"Hmm." Leo tilts his head back to finish off his beer, then sets the glass down. When he doesn't offer anything else, I glare at him.

"I know Maddy better than you. There's no way she thought I was about to…to *propose* to her or something."

Leo nods but still doesn't respond. We're at The Rusty Tavern, his favourite pub, and the crowd is basically the opposite of Harper's Bar: stoic bearded men sipping beer in silence.

"I mean, fine," I say finally, unable to bear the noise of my own thoughts. "We weren't exactly on the same page. Maybe I made some assumptions about polyamory *in general*. But I know there's no way Maddy's been secretly pining for me for years and I just missed it. I'm not that clueless."

At last, Leo clears his throat. "I don't think she's been pining for you for years."

"*Thank* you!" I cry, earning a scowl from a burly man in a beanie down the bar.

Leo holds up his hand. "But that doesn't mean you aren't clueless, Bracha. Like I said yesterday, there's a reason Maddy's your only repeat visitor."

"And like *I* said, I'm not madly in love with her and totally unaware of it," I retort.

Leo heaves a sigh. "That's not exactly what I was implying."

"Then what are you implying?" I fix him with a stare, then catch myself sliding off my stool. Leo grabs my arm and chuckles as I shuffle back into place.

"Never mind," he says. "You're a mess, cous."

I stare at my half-empty glass. "She said there isn't a single woman in Australia who could live up to my expectations," I mumble. "Maybe she's right."

Leo's brows shoot up. "Oh? Are we revising the list?"

"What? No!" I give him an incredulous look. "The list isn't the problem. It's the sample pool. I need to widen the search."

Leo lets out an absurdly loud shot of laughter. "Ah, I see. Australia couldn't possibly have the perfect nine-point woman so it's time to look overseas."

Maybe it's the beer but I'm warming to the idea. "Hey, Victoria keeps pushing me to take leave. Do some traveling. It's not the worst idea."

"I can't believe I'm saying this, but I agree," Leo says slowly. "New York, Paris, Buenos Aires, Budapest—"

"Leo, it's winter on the other side of the world and I hate the snow," I remind him and he rolls his eyes.

"It's not about the weather, it's about the women."

Leo pulls out his phone. "Statistically speaking, there are plenty of places where you're more likely to meet the perfect wife."

I gaze at him blearily as he starts a Google search. He's right. Sydney's clubs haven't found me my perfect woman, so an overseas trip with this *list* will.

In the back of my mind, the sober version of me is yelling in protest. *You don't need time off work, and you definitely don't need to fuck off around the globe!*

But I don't want to listen to sober me right now.

I raise my hand and the bartender glances over at me. "Four shots of vodka, please!" I call. Fluent in drunk-speak, the bartender nods and grabs the shot glasses from the shelf.

I fish the list out of my pocket, spread it out on the bar and grab a fistful of cocktail napkins. "Alright, I'm in," I tell Leo. "Let's upgrade the plan."

Chapter Three

Mum's coffee pot is ancient. It's cumbersome. It's noisy. And the coffee it brews on the "extra-strong" setting could strip paint off a car.

I sip it slowly, eyes closed, hands clasped around the mug. My temples are throbbing, and there's a dull ache in the back of my head. I rarely drink, and I rarely mix drinks, but last night got messy. Exhibit A: the half-crumpled cocktail napkins covered in Venn diagrams and equations, all in Leo's familiar loopy handwriting.

My gaze falls on one napkin, which simply reads OH CANADA???? A vague memory surfaces, Leo and I trying to sing a few lines of Canada's national anthem as the only other customer enjoying last call at the tavern threw some change on the bar and left in disgust.

Now, I roll my eyes. As if I'd actually go overseas at a time like this. Not when the ED is in the middle of our busiest season, my best-friend is pissed at me, and I have an ever-growing "to fix" list for the house.

And an about-to-be-freed brother who has his eye on it.

A knock comes at the front door, followed by a singsong, "Knock-knock!"

I turn too quickly and stifle a groan at the renewed pounding in my head. "Door's open!" I call as loudly as I can bear, gathering up the cocktail napkins. Aunt Aggie appears in the kitchen entryway as I shove the napkins into a drawer. Her entire upper body is obscured by the overstuffed shopping bags in her arms. When she sets them on the table, I see she's wearing a forest green sweater dress that clings to her curves, with a chunky gold necklace nestled between her cleavage. Her hair is freshly cut and dyed her signature plum colour—or rather, the exact shade of her favourite shiraz, as she instructs her hairdresser.

"Brachaleh!" Aunt Aggie exclaims, pulling me into a bone-crushing hug. I can practically feel my brain rattling in my skull as she kisses both my cheeks, adding one more for good measure.

I kiss both her cheeks in return, then pull away. "I didn't know you were coming today," I say as Aunt Aggie sets to work unpacking the groceries.

She clicks her tongue. "Well, I didn't have much of a choice now, did I? You know I love my dear sister, but her rooms are filled to the brim with ghosts this time of year. So chatty! So persistent! Only answer is to keep tidying, you know, to rid them so she may rest in peace."

I smile as she busies herself putting away the butter and eggs. Since shiva ended, my aunt has been coming over more days than not to "tidy up," which is a thinly veiled excuse for going through her sister's things and reminiscing.

"And where's my other little cherub?" she asks.

"Working," I reply, sinking back into my chair.

Sipping my coffee, I watch my aunt turn the kitchen into the site of a semi-exorcism while keeping up a steady stream of chatter. The thing with Agatha is that everything is sporadic, and nothing is predictable. When Leo was twelve, Aunt Aggie packed up and joined an Outback Nunnery in the middle of Australia. This is despite the fact that she's Jewish and God would have to be her second husband after one kid and a divorce. Since then, her conversations with God have extended to all the afterlife.

After the nunnery, it was ballet school—yes, at age thirty, she truly believed she could still achieve fame and glory en pointe. When that failed, it had nothing to do with her feet and everything to do with the fact that she kept bringing baked goods to class. After all that "strict" dieting, Aunt Aggie became a cafe assistant—something we all thought might actually stick, seeing as she loves to cook. But her talents were, in her words, "far too advanced for the clientele of Surry Hills," and she quit two weeks in.

After Mum's funeral, Aunt Aggie told us she was going away for a week of self-reflection at Bella's Beauty House. I pointed out that Bella's is only a ten-minute drive down the road, to which my aunt argued that "proximity to the house is not a spiritual impediment to cleansing the soul."

Now, here she is getting out the skillet and slicing tomatoes, and I realise I can't remember the last time I ate.

I'm a doctor. I know what shock looks like, and I'm smart enough to recognise that I'm in it. I forget my Mum is dead and call out to her when I am in the house. I don't eat because I don't feel hungry. I don't sleep at normal hours and don't remember how I get to sleep when I finally do. I tell myself everything is fine, and everything *is* fine. Because I don't need to accept that I'm in shock. I can tell myself to just keep going because that's what I do. Plan and persist. Persistence is key. Keep moving forward to the next goal. It's how I operate. Keep planning, set goals, achieve them. Tick Tick.

A text pops up from Leo. *FYI Mum's coming back today. Something about ghosts? Staying for good this time, or so she says.*

I shake my head and smile. *Thanks for the warning but it's a bit late. She's already cooking.*

Must be torturous for you, comes the immediate response.

At least I'll get a good meal.

Don't you have better things to do?

Such as?

Such as BOOK A FLIGHT?

"Eggs are up!" Aunt Aggie slides a plate loaded with a rye bagel, a well-done omelette, grilled tomatoes, and mushrooms in front of me. I pocket my phone and pull the plate closer. My stomach rumbles and I ignore the collection of pots, pans and dishes on the bench.

"Thanks, Aggie."

"Anytime, sweetie."

As I eat, Aunt Aggie picks up a folded piece of paper I missed on the bench. "What's this?" She asks, holding it out so I can see my list. "You taking out a personal ad, babka?"

I nearly choke on a mouthful of eggs. "No."

Aunt Aggie settles into the chair opposite mine and pulls off the Tiffany's glasses Mum bought her last year. She taps the list. "This isn't the girl you were seeing last month, I know that much. Not the brightest of the bunch."

She's talking about Maddy. Aggie has a deep suspicion of anyone who didn't spend their teenage years reading Henrik Ibsen or Oscar Wilde under a blanket fort, contemplating the tragedy of the human condition. But Maddy has her own smarts, she moved out at seventeen and became the youngest bank manager at her branch—solving *actual* human conditions, like "How do I approve your overdraft?"

I tear off a huge bite of bagel to avoid responding and wonder how Maddy is doing.

"Hmm, I think I see your problem, Brachaleh." Aunt Aggie sets down the list. "This is far too long. You should only have one point on here."

"Oh? And what's that?"

She flashes a smile. "Rich."

"What?"

"*Rich*, bubka. Wealth. Money. Lots of it. You can endure any other flaws when you're sitting in your luxury Mercedes EV with your Christian Dior visor. And don't forget the leather seats."

I chuckle as I take another sip of coffee. "Hate to break it to you but I don't think Mercedes even makes an EV."

Aggie winks. "Bet they do if the price is right."

After I finish eating, Aggie and I clean up the kitchen before getting to work and by work, I mean me trying to organise Mum's belongings into boxes for storage or donations while each item sends Aggie off into another long-winded story.

It's slow progress to say the least.

An hour later, I'm going through Mum's dresser and half-listening to Aggie, who discovered a pair of unworn red heels in a box in the back of the closet that triggered a memory of some fundraising gala she and Mum went to years ago. My mum had this whole classy-academic-meets-corporate-powerhouse vibe— like someone who could publish a thesis and close a deal before lunch. She was just 21 when she met my dad; he was a 35-year-old who wooed her with persistence that bordered on stalking. When she finally caved, she forced him to shave his thick-coiled hair and beard which made him look ten years younger. Mum was the quintessential bossy "hard to get" type, but she had a knack for knowing things you hadn't even figured out about yourself yet.

The top right dresser drawer is stuffed with notebooks and planners and I can't help but flip through some of them, my chest tightening at the sight of Mum's perfectly legible script. In the very back is a vaguely familiar blue journal, but I don't fully recognise it until I see my own sloppy handwriting in glittering blue ink.

Her breath smells like mint and her hair smells like coconuts. She has a little mole over her mouth, just like Drew Barrymore. Her laugh is kind of mellow and it literally makes my legs turn into mush. She's almost two years older than me but I think it's okay because everyone says I'm mature for 14.

I haven't said this out loud yet but...I THINK I'M IN LOVE WITH NAOMI KAPLAN.

"Holy shit," I whisper, my eyes moving to the bottom of the page. To my horror, there's a giant heart with the initials NK and BC, which are added together to equal (what else?) 4Eva.

Of course, I remember Naomi vividly. No one forgets their first crush, and Naomi was my first in a few other ways, too. We met at the kibbutz in Israel, where I went to school. I think about her every once in a while.

What I'd forgotten until right this moment was the *feelings*. How absolutely stupidly head over heels I'd been for her and it's all right here in this diary, pure humiliation in sparkly blue ink. I fight the urge to grab a pen, cross out *literally* and replace it with *figuratively*.

I flip through the pages, stopping on one where the ink is smeared. I can barely make out a few words—*over, Australia, begged, New York*—and realise with a fresh wave of embarrassment that the ink is smudged thanks to my adolescent tears. Naomi's family had moved to New York, while mine was heading for Australia. I'd pleaded with Naomi not to end things, believing in my foolish teen heart that a long-distance relationship was totally possible.

Gazing at my own words it dawns on me that I've never felt about any woman the way I felt about Naomi. Which meant I'd never experienced the heartbreak fourteen-year-old Bracha had suffered either.

Empirical proof that logic trumped romance

when it came to finding a partner.

I close the diary with a snap and begin organising the drawer. But my mind keeps wandering back to Naomi, the kibbutz, and my childhood in Israel. I'd been devastated about the move at the time. But now, it was hard to imagine what my life would have been like if we hadn't moved to Australia and left the ongoing wars. Our family's problems hadn't really started until after the move. That was when Mum and Dad had really started arguing and it was when Eli had fallen in with the wrong crowd. Both Mum and Dad regretted leaving, always saying it was a mistake. Makes me wonder why they didn't stay together.

I'm surprised to feel a brief surge of compassion for my brother. Teenagers are selfish creatures, and at the time, I'd only thought about my own suffering. But Eli had said goodbye to friends in Israel, too, and I know the divorce three years later had been as hard on him as it had been on me. We hadn't leaned on each other. I'd put all my energy into making plans for my future, propelled by the desire to never feel that kind of instability again, that kind of heartbreak.

Eli had put all his energy into doing—and eventually, selling—drugs.

As I tuck the last planner into the drawer, a slip of paper falls out. I pick it up, but I'm so lost in thought that it takes a full minute before I realise what I'm looking at.

A plane ticket.

I stare at the faded print in disbelief. Not just a plane ticket. A ticket to Ben Gurion.

To Tel Aviv.

When did Mum buy this? *Why* did she buy this? I knew for a fact she'd never gone back to Israel not even for a visit. Whipping out my phone, I Google the flight number and my breath catches. It was just last year, a few months before her health took a turn for the worse.

My mind is reeling. "Aggie?" I call, and my aunt pokes her head out of the closet.

"Yes, bubka?"

"Was Mum planning a trip to Israel last year?"

Aunt Aggie's brow furrows as she squints at the ticket I'm holding up. Then her expression clears, and she sighs. "Ah that, I'd almost forgotten."

I try to ignore a stab of hurt. "Why didn't she tell me?"

"She was planning on telling you!" Aggie said quickly, stepping out of the closet. I realise she's wearing Mum's favourite silk robe. "It was a rather spontaneous decision. We'd been out for drinks talking about ways to shake her out of her rut."

Her rut. I press my lips together tightly. My aunt knew full well that Mum's *rut* was clinical depression. It had taken me over a year to realise she spoke about it so dismissively not because she didn't take it seriously but because it was her way of coping with her sister's illness.

"We ended up talking about the happiest times of our lives and why they were so happy," Aggie continues, twirling a lock of wine-coloured hair around her finger. "Of course, mine was the kibbutz in the 70s. Such an enlightening experience. So many men…tanned, muscular, built like—"

"Aggie," I say, trying to hide my impatience.

"Sorry." She flashes me an easy grin. "So, we decided a trip home was just what the doctor ordered for your mother. Still, I couldn't believe when she showed me that ticket. That she actually went through with it, you know? But then—" Aggie hesitates. "Well. Eli was arrested."

I flinch as if she'd flung the words at me. *Of course,* I think, wondering how I hadn't made the connection sooner.

Aggie is off on another tangent about her kibbutz experience, but I tune her out. The ticket in my hand is yet another example of how Eli's selfish choices ruined my mother's life. Ruined *our* lives. I get why Mum decided not to take the trip after his arrest but I can't believe she didn't tell me about it. Mum told me everything.

At least, I thought she did.

My phone buzzes, pulling me from these thoughts. I stare down at the Google calendar notification Dad has just sent me, and the shock from Dad's text jolts me more than the shock I am already in.

Eli's release date, along with a smiley emoji. It's two weeks away.

I swipe the notification away, trying to ignore the way my hand is trembling. I don't understand either of my parents right now. Dad's excitement over my brother's early release, Mum's secret, cancelled trip—

I gaze at the plane ticket. *Ben Gurion, Tel Aviv, Israel.* I think about all the cocktail napkins covered in statistics and diagrams and potential places to meet the perfect Jewish wife, and despite everything, I suddenly want to laugh.

Opening the messages app, I send Leo a text.

Israel. Statistically speaking…

His response comes seconds later.

YAASSSSS!

***

Fifteen minutes later, I'm in my room searching for flights to Tel Aviv. I can hear the sounds of Aggie belting out the chorus to *Valerie* down the hall, and I can't help but wonder what she'd say if she knew what I was doing.

A little voice whispers in the back of my mind, *what* are *you doing, Bracha?*

Spontaneity isn't my thing. I make plans, and I follow them through. But my head is swimming with my own childish ramblings about my first love at the kibbutz, and the secret trip home my Mum never got to take and my brother's impending release and whatever it is he wants with this house, and I need to get away from all of this.

Maybe Israel has the answers.

Maybe my future wife is there. Statistically, it's my best option.

I open Maps in a new tab, centre on Tel Aviv, and search for hostels. After a minute or so of scrolling through photos, a brightly coloured mural catches my eye: a tanned woman with her head tilted back to soak in rays of the sun, vines thick with flowers growing out of her head and wrapping around her torso. Something about it makes me smile and I click through to the website.

A chat window pops up at the bottom.

Hello! My name's Dani. Let me know if you have any questions or need help booking a stay at Beit Yam.

Ocean House, sounds like just what I need. I chew my lip, then type back:

Any accommodations available ASAP?

While I wait for the response, I check out the photo gallery. Bunk beds neatly made with crisp white sheets, a clean but sparsely stocked kitchen, a large common room with bright blue sofas and several round tables with plastic chairs. And those murals are everywhere, covering the walls, the shelves, even parts of the ceiling.

A new message appears in the chat box. *Definitely! Can I get your name?*

Bracha, I type. *I have a few more questions. Is there a cap on how long visitors can stay?*

Depends on the visitor.

I blink. *Cheeky chatbot.*

Not a chatbot. I work here. You can stay as long as you aren't that guy who tries to brew his own beer in the washing machine at two in the morning.

I find myself grinning as I respond. *True story?*

100%. Any other questions?

Yes. I pause. *Do you supply toilet paper?*

Of course.

Scented or unscented?

Scented. Lavender.

Do you provide blackout curtains?

No. We used to but then we stopped growing mushrooms.

I let out a choke of laughter. *Sheet laundry.*

I highly recommend it, yes.

I wasn't finished, I type. *Is it changed regularly, or is it my responsibility?*

Are you asking me to change your sheets, Bracha?

Not you specifically but…staff.

There's a pause. Then:

I suppose if the price is right. Would you like me to make your bed every morning?

I suspect you're being sarcastic but honestly? Yes.

That gets a laughing emoji. I feel strangely proud as if getting a chuckle from this random hostel employee is an accomplishment.

An email notification pops up and I switch tabs. My mouth goes dry when I see a response from the lawyer. Holding my breath, I open the message, but my hopes are quickly dashed as I skim his reply.

"Demonstrated exceptional good behaviour in his prison report," I murmur, my shoulders tensing as I read. "Clearly of sound mind…withholding his inheritance would be illegal…estate must be paid out within six months…fuck me."

I jab at my keyboard to close the tab. *Good behaviour my arse.* My brother was the master at sucking up, though. He got away with all kinds of things when we were kids just by flashing his best puppy dog eyes and offering a quiet "I'm sorry" with an undercurrent of sarcasm that apparently only I could detect.

My skin feels hot and prickly, and my palms are sweating. I have the urge to run. Literally stand up and flee my house and get as far away from *this,* this dead Mum, arsehole brother, confusing father, hurt friend pile of crap that is currently my life.

"You know what?" I say out loud. "Let's do it."

I focus on my screen where the hostel website is still open and there's a new message from Dani.

I'll be sure to fold your sheets down to exactly 45 degrees.

Deal, I reply. *Got a bed available in two days?*

Chapter Four

After nearly twenty-four straight hours of travel, during which I've lost nine hours and all sense of time, I'm sitting in a taxi, pulling away from Ben Gurion and staring at the dreary grey sky through the window. It's December, which in Australia means beaches and sun-kissed skin, but here in Tel Aviv, it means gloomy grey clouds and a damp chill in the air. I've always hated winter.

I can already feel the doubt creeping in. My Israeli passport had expired along with most of my Hebrew. I had to use my Australian passport coming in. I flip open my passport to find the three-month stay date stamped on my visa. It reminds me of why I'm doing this. I have three months to find the perfect wife.

And that's all I need.

I tuck the passport away and pull out my phone. I texted Maddy a few times before I left, but still no response. The only new message is from Aggie: *If you end up at a kibbutz make sure your future "someone special" owns it!*

It could be the jet lag, but I'm surprised to feel a wave of sadness. I can't believe I'm doing this. Everyone was so supportive and not nearly as surprised at my announcement that I'd booked a flight to Tel Aviv. Victoria would've thrown a bon voyage party if she'd had the time. Leo promised to keep up with the house maintenance in my absence. Dad…

Well, Dad doesn't know about this trip. Yet. Usually I tell him all my plans and I meant to call him, but it turns out packing for a last-minute trip around the globe to find a wife takes a lot of time.

I check my email. Nothing from my lawyers—I never responded to the message about Eli because what can I say to that kind of incompetence? —but there's a new message from the hostel.

Hi Bracha,

Looking forward to meeting you. I wanted to check in and see if I can assist with anything else during your stay. Would you like to book any non-animal, food-free tours? A midnight yoga session? Just say the word!

Dani

I find myself smiling as I swipe the app closed.

The taxi turns, and suddenly, the Tayelet spreads outside my window. Never mind the season, never mind that the waters of the Mediterranean look more grey than blue, never mind that the beach isn't swarming with sunbathers—the sight still made my thoughts pause. Memories I haven't thought of in years begin to swim to the surface: building sandcastles with Mum, racing Eli out into the water with our bodyboards in an ongoing competition to see who could catch the biggest waves (which is near impossible as there are no waves here because of the breakers), Dad sipping steaming hot espressos even in the dead of summer.

I'm startled to realise my eyes are swimming with tears, and I brush them away hastily.

Five minutes later, I'm pulling my suitcase out of

the back of the taxi. The hostel is as colourful in person as it was online, a three-story structure painted bright yellow with blocks of green and blue. Beit Yam is spelled out in Hebrew as well as English, both in fonts that wouldn't be out of place in a kindergarten classroom. I take one last, long whiff of the briny sea air before heading through the glass double doors.

"Welcome!" a short, round man with a shiny bald head booms the moment I step inside. He's standing behind the counter and beaming as if a celebrity just stepped into the hostel, rather than a sleep-deprived half-Australian, half-Israeli, with a terrible case of plane hair. "I'm Omer, the owner, and I'm delighted you're here. Accommodations for one?"

"Yes. No." I pinch the bridge of my nose willing myself to wake up. "I mean, I already made a reservation online for a private room for Bracha Cohen."

"Ah, wonderful!" Omer's thick fingers fly over the iPad on the counter. "Yes, I see here that Dani helped you book your stay!"

Before I can respond, the door to the office opens. "What did I do?" A woman wearing red overalls over a Nirvana T-shirt steps out, and against all laws of physics, the outfit does wonders for her hips. Auburn hair tumbles over her shoulders in waves and her hazel eyes sparkle as they meet mine.

Now I'm awake.

"Dani!" Omer exclaims, handing her the iPad. "This is Bracha. I just got her checked in, if you wouldn't mind showing her around?"

"Bracha Cohen," Dani says, her Israeli accent bouncing through the air. "Glad you made it."

"Me too," I reply automatically, only vaguely aware of Omer heading back into the office. A light smattering of freckles covers Dani's cheeks, as I catch her hair trailing down her neck and over her collarbone. I can't help but wonder where the trail leads under her shirt, then shake the thought off.

Physically, she hits more than a few of the requirements on my list. But up close, I can see she's young. Really young. Her thirties are a distant future, not a pressing reality. *Sorry, Dani. You don't quite make the cut.*

"Sorry about the blackout curtains," Dani says playfully as she leads me through the lobby. "I pitched the idea to Omer, but seeing as most of our guests get back to their rooms around three in the morning very drunk, we thought maybe pitch-blackness was a lawsuit waiting to happen."

"Fair enough. I brought a sleep mask, anyway. And earplugs."

"Very smart," Dani replies seriously. "Can't sacrifice that beauty sleep."

Her tone is teasing. I fight the urge to run my fingers through my flattened hair and fail to think of a clever response. A hot shower and clean clothes would go a long way toward restoring my flirting abilities.

"Kitchen's right here, fully stocked," Dani says, gesturing to the entrance. "Do you eat breakfast?"

"Of course. I generally eat at eight, noon, four,

and eight every day."

"Really?"

"On the dot." I spot a stainless-steel refrigerator, a large microwave, and no fewer than three coffee pots on the counter.

"It works," Dani tells me. "But if you want a really good coffee, I recommend The Galya next door."

"Noted."

She taps her chin and studies me. "Let's see…double espresso with sugar?"

"Close," I say with a grin. "Long black. No sugar."

"Cool. And if you're planning on keeping actual food here, I suggest labelling them," Dani adds. "And potentially booby-trapping them. We occasionally get some guests who think nothing of borrowing food with hands that don't stay in place—if you know what I mean."

"Okay. Any booby trap recommendations?" I ask as she leads me past the showers.

"Mouse traps," she replies immediately.

"Cruel!"

"To mice, yes." Dani shoots me another grin. "To that Canadian hippie who tried to steal my imported cheese last week? Not cruel enough."

Dammit. I like her.

As we near the end of the hall, the sound of boisterous chatter reaches my ears. "Must be the common room," I guess.

"It is," Dani says. "Common room—and bar. It's a popular spot."

She isn't kidding. The space is easily the size of the

entire first floor of Mum's house. A tiki-style bar takes up the entire left wall, with gold fairy lights strung around the shelves lined with green glass bottles. Sofas and loveseats in funky plaid upholstery are sectioned off, creating four distinctive zones for smaller groups to hang out. Round tables and stools are clustered closer to the bar, while an air hockey table and two pool tables are clearly the main features, taking up the centre of the room.

Nearly every seat is taken with at least a dozen more grungy backpackers shooting pool. Two dudes with the kind of bleached blonde curls and weathered skin that can only come from surfing are locked in a heated air hockey match.

"Nice." I glance at Dani. "Care to have a quick drink?"

Her eyebrows arch, and I suddenly remember she's an employee.

"You're working, never mind," I say hastily. "Sorry. Jet lag brain."

Dani laughs. "Believe me, it wouldn't be the first time I had a beer on the job. Maybe—" She pauses and glances at her phone screen which is lit up. Then she lets out an honest to goodness squeal. I watch in amusement as she does a little happy dance while typing a response.

"Good news?"

"Hmm?" Dani looks up, her face practically glowing. "Oh. Yeah, my girlfriend's gonna FaceTime me after my shift. I haven't actually seen her face in a week."

Girlfriend? I ignore the way my stomach sinks. "Is she out of town?"

Dani lets out a dry laugh. "You could say that. She lives in New York."

I make a face. "Long distance?"

"Yeah, it's a challenge," Dani says with a shrug. "But you know. You do what you have to do."

And with that, Dani is officially out of consideration as a contender for my perfect wife. If her age and lack of career weren't enough, her impracticality is a total dealbreaker. Never mind how good her arse looks in those overalls.

Dani shows me to my room, which is roughly the size of Mum's closet, before returning to the lobby. I drop off my bag and head to the kitchen to fill my travel mug to the brim with strong, black coffee, then head to the bar.

It's even more crowded now. I spot one empty seat at a small table where a couple sit drinking bottled beer. The woman catches me eyeing the chair and smiles, waving me over.

"You don't mind?" I ask, already pulling the chair out.

"No. Sit!" she replies, her dangly earrings brushing her bare shoulders. "I'm Katya and this is Josh."

"Bracha. Nice to meet you."

Josh leans forward, flashing a grin. "Is that an Aussie accent I detect?"

"I suppose so," I say. "Although I grew up here."

We fall into an easy conversation. Katya is

stunning, with high cheekbones and reddish-brown hair that tumbles down her back. She's wearing a long, floral dress and I can't help but notice her feet are bare beneath the table. Her Russian accent gives me the impression that the cold does not bother her even the slightest. It doesn't take long for me to figure out they aren't actually a couple but two strangers who met recently here at the hostel. Except, judging from the way Josh looks at Katya, that might change soon enough. I wouldn't blame her for going for it, either. Josh has curly dark hair tied up in a man bun, a scruffy five-o'clock shadow, and the kind of smile that doesn't know how to be anything other than flirtatious. He's wearing a singlet and shorts with flip flops, a look that would probably be deemed lazy, but with his build, it's sexy.

By the time my mug is empty, I've learned that Josh has a teaching degree from NYU and speaks Arabic and Hebrew. He is looking for a job now that he has moved to Tel Aviv. He lives a few blocks from Beit Yam and hangs out here to get away from his creepy roommate. (Although, reading between the lines, I'm pretty sure his real reason is the constant come-and-go flow of pretty girls like Katya.)

Katya served in the Army after school in the North of Israel, but otherwise, she's a hippie if I've ever met one. Zero ambition, total drifter, free spirit, planning to buy a one-way ticket to India—basically, the opposite of me. I can't help but like her. She reminds me a bit of Aggie. Case in point: she's living at the hostel for free in exchange for massaging Omer.

And I can tell from her earnest, wide-eyed expression that she actually means *massage*.

"Alright, Bracha, it's your turn." Katya turns to me expectantly. "Why did you leave the Garden of Eden in the middle of all that glorious heat to come to a frigid desert? It's not a mere vacation."

Her bluntness catches me off guard, especially after weeks of everyone I know gently poking at the grief I've worked so hard to pack away. So, I respond honestly.

"To find the perfect wife."

Katya's eyes widen, and Josh whistles. "Are you serious?" he asks.

"Very." I'm enjoying their reactions. "I'm here for three months. Phase one, date like mad until I find an ideal prospect, ideally in one month. Phase two, take another month or so to romance the hell out of her. Phase three, bring her back to Australia and organise a massive family wedding. It's what my Mum would've wanted."

I stop, annoyed with myself for letting that slip out.

Katya tilts her head. "Oh, dear. How long ago did she pass?"

"A little over a month." I pick up my mug, remember it's empty, and set it back down. "I've always been kind of a serial dater. Nothing serious. Mum wanted to see me settle down with someone. And after she…well, after, I realised I wanted that, too."

"Question." Josh raises his hand like this is school.

"Why go around the world? No good options at home? Because I've had my fair share of encounters with Aussie ladies and I beg to differ."

I picture Maddy and ignore a flash of guilt. "Statistical probability," I tell him, pulling the list out of my pocket. Josh and Katya lean together to read as I explain the logic behind *The List*.

Josh finishes first and gives me a sceptical look. "This is insane."

"I think it's brave." Katya beams at me. "And romantic. Going after what you want like this."

"Are you sure it's what you want, though?" Josh elbows me. "From one player to another, I have to say the 'date like mad' part of your plan sounds like fun. Maybe just stick to that? The single life is pretty great."

I smile. "Yeah, it's been great—but it's also been close to a decade. I'm ready for a change, you know? This woman," I add, tapping the list. "Once I meet her, I'll be all in."

For the briefest of seconds, Josh's gaze flicks over to Katya. "Yeah, alright," he says, nodding. "I hear you. Consider me your wingman."

Katya tips her head back to drain her bottle, which she slams on the table. "Me too," she announces. "How about we start looking tonight? There's a great club close by."

I glance at my watch, startled to realise it's nearly eight o'clock. But any jet lag I'd felt earlier has been banished by strong coffee and new friends.

Josh and Katya are looking at me expectantly. I

glance down at my grungy plane clothes.

"Give me an hour to clean up," I tell them. "I'll meet you in the lobby?"

"Perfect!" Katya claps her hands in delight. "Tonight, we find Bracha's wife!"

Chapter Five

One boiling hot shower later, I'm feeling human again. I unpack in record time, then pull on a pair of charcoal black jeans, a plain white T-shirt, and boots. I run a bit of wax through my hair and give myself a quick glance in the mirror.

"Not bad," I tell my reflection.

In the lobby, I spot Dani on a short stepladder attempting to hang one side of a banner that reads Новым годом!

"Little early for New Year's decor, isn't it?" I ask, moving over to help her.

She grins without looking down. "You read Russian?"

"Nah, I've just seen my share of Novi God stuff," I reply. "Here, I've got it."

I step onto the other side of the ladder, take the end of the banner and tape it to the wall so that it's even with the other side. When I finish and face Dani, we're practically nose to nose. She looks me up and down, the corner of her mouth quirking up.

"You clean up pretty good," she says in bubbly Hebrew.

I can smell peppermint on her breath. "I try." I reply back.

Dani steps off the ladder, and I reluctantly do, too. "You speak Hebrew?"

"A little." I murmur trying to hide my poor

intonation.

She eyes me smiling. "Big plans tonight?"

"Yes, actually." I watch as she rips open a plastic bag of silver streamers. "I met a few people at the bar and we're going out to find me a wife."

Dani pauses, eyeing me. "Did you say find a *wife*?"

And so I launch into a more abbreviated version of why I'm here. When I finish, Dani's hazel eyes are as round as coins.

"So, to clarify," she says slowly in perfect English, "you're planning on meeting, dating, and proposing to someone in the next three months?"

"Two months," I correct her. "The third month should be mostly about actual wedding preparations."

"I can't tell if you're joking."

"Why? What's funny about marriage?"

"Nothing," Dani says quickly. "Marriage is great. It's just you might not meet a woman who meets your criteria and then what?"

There isn't a single woman in Australia who could live up to your ridiculous expectations. I shake off thoughts of Maddy and clear my throat.

"Of course, there's never a guarantee," I reply. "But statistically speaking, the probability of meeting my ideal woman is highest here based on Tel Aviv's demographics and the one variable in my control is how many women I meet. Obviously, the more I meet, the higher the odds I'll find one that fits the list. Which is why I'm getting started tonight."

Dani listens, chewing her lip. She almost looks … not worried exactly but concerned. "Well, sounds like you've given this a lot of thought."

"Of course I have." I frown slightly. "Marriage is a big deal. Doesn't it warrant serious thought?"

"Of course it does," Dani replies. "But, you know, usually that serious thought comes after you've actually met someone."

"Which is why most romantic relationships end up being a waste of time," I point out. "You're with someone for months, years even, then realise there's no future. And you're back to square one. My way is much more logical."

"Interesting point."

Something in her tone irritates me. "I suppose you've given serious thought to whether you want to marry Miss. Long Distance?"

Dani's expression softens. "Her name is Riley, and yes, of course I have. If and when she proposes, I'd move to New York."

"And you think she will?"

"Actually——" Dani says very matter-of-fact. "She's coming here for New Year's, and I have a feeling she's planning something."

"A proposal?"

"Maybe." Dani shrugs and I can tell she's trying to hide her excitement. "She's been super busy with work lately——new boss, that kind of thing. We don't get to talk as often, and we miss each other, and she's been different lately. Secretive, you know? I think she wants it to be a surprise, so I haven't said anything."

"Well, perhaps we'll both be getting engaged by the new year," I say.

A wide smile splits Dani's cheeks and it's so pure, so filled with an innocent sort of joy, that I almost feel protective of her. Because if this Riley *isn't* planning a proposal, it's clearly going to break Dani's heart.

***

Three hours and four clubs later, my brain has completely checked out.

Normally, after a night like Leo and I had just a few days ago, it'd be months before I touched another drop of alcohol, but we hadn't been in the first club two minutes before Josh handed me a shot glass filled with something spicy and smokey. After a few of those, Katya ordered a round of rum and cokes. I tried to decline, but when an email notification from my lawyer popped up on my phone that began, *"We received a message from your brother's representation requesting a call…"* suddenly alcohol sounded like a fine idea indeed. Fizzy cocktails at the next club helped wash away annoying questions like *how does Eli even have money for a lawyer?* and an icy larger at the third club did the trick when it dawned on me that perhaps Dad was paying for his representation.

Club number four is called Loops, and I turn my phone off before strutting inside, flanked by Katya and Josh. I'm not here to think about Eli. I'm here to find the perfect woman.

My new friends, as it turns out, are fantastic wingmen. Sure, the first few girls Katya sent my way were barely out of high school and, therefore, instant disqualifications, while Josh had introduced me to more than a few straight women who were clearly more interested in him than me. But they were improving as the night went on.

The bass thrums in my chest as I move across the dance floor, my gaze locked on a pretty blonde in a Panama hat who, I have to admit, looks a bit like Maddy. Just as I realise, she's with a lanky guy rocking impressive sideburns, someone taps on my shoulder. I turn and find myself face to face with a stunning brunette wearing a white blazer with a plunging neckline and absolutely nothing beneath it. My eyes roam down her cleavage and stomach before returning to meet her gaze.

"Bracha?" she asks in a throaty voice, her words thick with an Israeli accent. "They call me Shiran. Your friends thought we might … like to dance."

She gestures over to the bar, where Josh and Katya are huddled together and watching us expectantly. Grinning, I turn back to the magnificent woman in front of me.

"They thought right," I say.

Shiran smiles widely and I can't help thinking her cheekbones could cut glass. Turning, I flash Josh and Katya a thumbs up before Shiran takes my hand and pulls me deeper into the crowd.

For the next forty-five minutes, there's never more than an inch of air between our bodies. Her English is about as good as my Hebrew, but we manage to learn a little about one another over the thumping of the music. My skin buzzes pleasantly as she slides her hands around my waist and tells me about a recent ad campaign, she worked on for a men's cologne brand.

"I think I may never get rid of the smell," she jokes, moving in so I can smell her neck. The scent is a mix of cinnamon, bourbon, and campfire that sends a ripple of heat straight down my chest and deep into my stomach.

"I don't think that'd be the worst thing," I murmur, my lips brushing against her skin

When the music shifts into something more techno with a fast beat, Shiran pulls away and glances at her watch. "I should be going," she says. When she lifts her gaze to meet mine, I can already see the answer to the question I'm about to ask.

"Can I see you tomorrow?"

She smiles again. "I would like that. Coffee?"

"That sounds great," I reply. "How about The Galya, maybe around ten?"

"Perfect." Shiran gives me her phone number. After I enter it into my contacts, she moves forward and gives me a kiss on the cheek that lingers. I watch her saunter away, smiling like an idiot.

"Aw, what happened?" Josh appears at my side, closely followed by Katya. "I thought she was a sure thing."

"It looked like you two really hit it off," Katya added.

"We did," I tell them. "She gave me her number. We're meeting for coffee tomorrow."

Josh pulls a face. "I think you missed a step. You know, the one where you go back to her place?"

"The objective of tonight wasn't to get laid," I say, pulling out my phone. "It was to find a potential wife and set up a date. Mission accomplished."

"You're leaving?" Katya rests her head on Josh's shoulder and bats her eyelashes at me. "Already? You only got one number!"

I notice the way Josh snakes his arm around her waist. He catches my eye and gives me a sly look, and I swallow a laugh. Getting laid might not be my mission tonight, but it's definitely his.

"One's all I need," I tell Katya. "Besides, I don't want to show up for my first date with the woman I might marry looking like a jet-lagged hungover wreck, do I?"

"Fair point," Josh says. "Go get your beauty sleep."

I order a taxi as I weave my way through throngs of gyrating bodies. When I glance back, I spot Josh and Katya melded together in the middle of the dance floor. She's laughing as he whispers in her ear, his hands on her hips. They're cute together but it's such a mismatch.

I arrive back at the hostel fifteen minutes later, drunk and exhilarated. Dani isn't in the lobby—no one is, of course, seeing as its two in the morning—and I'm feeling chatty. Sinking into a plush armchair, I pull out my phone again. For the first time, I notice several missed calls from Dad. Frowning, I open FaceTime.

A few seconds later, Leo's face fills the screen. "Hey, what's up? Everything okay?"

"More than okay," I tell him, vaguely aware that my words are slightly slurred. "I went out with a few new friends and met someone."

Leo's eyebrows shoot up. "Oh?"

"Her name is…" I pause for dramatic effect. "Shiran. She's gorgeous, she's smart, she works in marketing—and we've got a date tomorrow."

"Nice."

"Nice?" I give him a mock offended look. "Leo, I'm telling you the story of how I met my wife so you can recount it in your best man's speech and all you can say is *nice*?"

It comes out louder than I intended, and Leo squints at me.

"You're drunk," he says. "So, I'll forgive you for this lapse in logic. But Bracha, the statistical probability of you meeting *the one* first is…well, next to nil."

I wave a dismissive hand and knock over the lamp on the end table next to my chair. "Crap," I mumble, righting it and dropping my phone in the process. When I pick it up, Leo looks amused but a bit concerned.

"You're *very* drunk."

"Meh." I can't argue with that. "Maybe. But I'm telling you, Shiran meets the criteria, Leo."

"I hope so," he says. "And I expect a full report tomorrow." There's a pause, then he adds: "On another topic, Aggie told me Eli's asking questions about the house … Bracha, why didn't you tell me?"

A dull throbbing starts behind my temples. I don't

want to think about Eli right now.

"Because there's nothing to tell," I say shortly. "I'll handle my brother, Leo."

"But—"

"I need to get my beauty sleep," I blurt out, remembering Josh's words. "Big day tomorrow. Future wife stuff. Talk to you later, okay?"

I hang up before he can respond and get to my feet. Once the lobby has stopped swaying, I slowly make my way toward my room. By the time I've brushed my teeth and crawled into bed, I've pushed my brother out of my mind. In no time at all, I sink into dreams of campfire cologne and cutting cheekbones.

Chapter Six

Sleep does little to restore my beauty.

I drag myself out of my hostel bed around nine o'clock and study myself in the mirror. The wax in my hair from last night, combined with a starchy, stiff pillowcase, has given me a look suggesting I've just been electrocuted. Dark circles beneath my eyes have me wondering if I need to dig out the concealer. What I really want is a nice, long morning run to get my adrenaline pumping before my date. But the way I'm feeling right now, I'd make it half way down the street before losing whatever's left in my stomach.

After a long, boiling hot shower and three cups of water from the bathroom tap, I head next door to The Galya. Immediately, I can see why Dani recommended the place. The rich, thick scent of espresso permeates the air, and the drinks menu features only the basics— black coffee, instant coffee, and something that translates as upside-down coffee, which is really just a cappuccino.

I order a black coffee and then grab a seat at a cosy table for two near the window. A mural near the door catches my eye, this one is of a pioneering kibbutz woman staring into the desert sun with a eucalyptus sapling in her palms. It's funny that the picture of drying Israeli swamps reminds me of my Australian home.

I sip my coffee, and the rich, smooth brew works

like a muscle relaxer. Through the window, I spot Shiran getting out of a taxi. She's wearing designer jeans with a blue silk top, her hair long and loose over her shoulders. I'm surprised at the flutter in my stomach—not attraction, although I definitely still feel that but actual nerves. I'm rarely nervous on dates.

But I feel the pressure of this one.

Shiran gives me a little wave as she walks in and I return it. I watch as she orders an upside-down coffee, then stand to pull out her chair as she approaches.

"Good morning," she says, flashing that beautiful smile. "You sleep okay?"

"Like a rock." When I see a flicker of confusion in her eyes, I add, "Very well, thanks. You?"

Watch your English, Bracha. No idioms. No slang.

"Sababa—I mean cool—thank you." Shiran takes a sip of coffee then sets her cup down and pulls out her phone. "The ad campaign I mentioned last night went out this morning. Want to see?"

"Of course!"

As she pulls up a video, I wonder if I should try speaking to her in Hebrew. Before arriving in Tel Aviv, I would have told anyone who asked that I was fluent, after all my dad still spoke in Hebrew on occasion, but it turns out that not speaking a language since childhood isn't great for maintaining the skill. Between Shiran and Josh, I'm starting to realise just how rusty I am.

For a moment, I wonder whether this is the tenth point on my list *English is one of her native languages*, but immediately I can hear Leo arguing that this would significantly reduce the statistical probability of finding a wife here.

There isn't a single woman in Israel who could live up to your ridiculous expectations, a voice that sounds remarkably like Maddy chides in the back of my mind.

In that moment, I decide this is actually an opportunity for a little self-improvement. I'll simply have to work on my Hebrew.

As Shiran launches into a story about filming the cologne commercial, I try to think of a way to steer the conversation towards family. More specifically, how interested is she in starting one? *Hey, do you want kids?* isn't exactly the kind of question most people ask on a first date. But it's also something that could make or break our relationship. And the clock is ticking—I can't waste time.

"Have you seen that commercial for perfume with the little girl getting into her mother's make-up?" I ask. It's not the best segue but it's all I've got at the moment. "I saw it a few times at the airport while I was waiting for my luggage."

Shiran's face brightens. "Oh, yes! I didn't work on it myself, but my company did."

Bingo. "It was adorable," I say. "And that girl was too cute."

"So gorgeous," Shiran agrees. "Nina from work told me…oh."

There's a subtle shift in her expression as her gaze flicks to the window. For the briefest of seconds, I catch a glimmer of excitement in her eyes. When I turn to look, I spot a bright blue Skoda shoving itself assertively into a ridiculously small car park on the crowded street. The driver emerges, a tall, bronzed man dressed in all Puma sports gear, which borders on commercial parody. He glowers at us through the glass and marches toward the entrance.

"Do you know him?" I ask.

Shiran clears her throat, "Ah, well. He's—"

Every head in the cafe swivels to stare as the man barges through the door like an angry soccer player entering the stadium.

"What are you thinking with this game?!" He exclaims in Hebrew.

He storms over to our table, launching into a tirade in rapid Hebrew. Shiran leaps to her feet, her cheeks flushed pink as she matches his verbal blows. My head spins as I catch words I vaguely recognise; he accuses Shiran of being *Haya be'seret* (living in a movie), as she counters by calling him a M*efager* (idiot). Puma man says the phrase S*tom da peh* at least three times, which was Eli's favourite phrase when we were kids literally translated to "Shut your mouth." When he tried to use it in English during our first week of school in Australia he got a week's detention.

It's only when Puma man levels his rant at me while gesturing at Shiran that I catch the word *Ishti and* my mind slowly catches up to what's going on.

My wife.

"Hang on." I stare up at Shiran in horror. "You're *married?*"

Puma gestures at the door; "*Kumi kumi*!! Get up, get up! We are leaving."

Shiran offers a half-smile and a shrug. I scoot my chair back to physically distance myself from her. If I could, I'd slide right out of the cafe.

"I didn't know," I tell Puma, holding both hands up in surrender. "I had no idea."

Puma rolls his eyes and switches to thickly accented English. "No no, this is not you. She plays games. We have fight, she go to make me jealous with women. She's crazy, she enjoys drama, like a movie."

I want to sink into the floor. Everyone in the cafe, including the barista, is openly staring. I say a silent prayer that no one is filming this to share on social media.

Shiran almost looks like she's enjoying herself. She says something to her husband in rapid Hebrew; I catch the word *mefager* again, and his scowl deepens.

"You don't respect," he spits out. "Not me and not yourself." To my horror, he turns to me for support. "Tell her. You want a real date, not this game."

My mouth opens and closes. Instinctively, I glance around the cafe, anything to avoid his gaze. Shiran snatches up her purse and snaps something in Hebrew that causes Puma to let out a harsh, humourless laugh.

"Tell her," He barks at me again.

"Hey, babe." Dani appears at my side wearing an expression of polite confusion. "Everything okay over here?"

She places a hand on my shoulder and squeezes. Finally, I manage to find my voice.

"Just a misunderstanding," I say, getting to my

feet. "I met a new friend for coffee, but her husband seems to think something else is going on."

"Oh." Dani slips her hand in mine and smiles at Puma. She speaks in Hebrew but clearly and slowly enough for me to understand every word. "This is my girlfriend. I assure you she has no interest in yours."

Shiran's face darkens and suddenly, she's not nearly as attractive. I arch an eyebrow at her, silently daring her to contradict Dani and confess to leading me on in front of her husband. Puma watches her, too. It might be my imagination, but I think maybe he's the one who's amused now.

Finally, Shiran shoulders her purse and storms out of the cafe with her head held high. Her husband follows, shaking his head and muttering to himself.

I let out a long, slow breath. It's only when I feel a squeeze that I realise Dani's hand is still in mine. I can't help feeling a little disappointed when she lets go and sinks into the chair Shiran was sitting in moments ago. She watches me as I sit, her eyes dancing.

"Was that prospective wife number one?" She asks, her voice low.

The other customers return to their own conversations but I'm acutely aware of the glances cast in my direction.

"It might have been," I admit.

The corner of Dani's mouth curls up, and I resist the urge to fan my too-warm face. "What are you doing here, anyway? Are you stalking me?" I try to sound teasing, but it still comes out a bit more accusatory than I'd like.

Before Dani can respond, the barista appears holding a to-go cup. "Your usual, Dani," he says, and I remember with a jolt of irritation that it was, in fact, Dani who recommended The Galya to me in the first place.

Dani beams up at him. "Thanks, David." She takes a long sip, clearly enjoying my discomfort. The barista heads back to the front and Dani leans back in her chair. "Definitely not stalking you. And you're welcome for saving your ass, by the way. That guy was ready to drag you to couple's therapy." She pauses, swirling the coffee around in her cup. "Or, I guess, thruple's therapy."

I roll my eyes. "Ha, ha. Aren't you going to be late for work?"

"My shift doesn't start until twelve," she replies. "I always grab a coffee here, then take a walk on the beach. It's kind of my morning routine." Dani hesitates for a moment. "Want to join me?"

I very much do. And not just because I'm desperate to get away from the whispers and stares.

A few minutes later, we're strolling down the Tayelet boardwalk. The chilly breeze and briny scent of seawater wash away the humiliation of what just happened.

"I used to come here with my grandfather when I was little," Dani says, gazing wistfully out at the grey-blue waves cresting on the rocks. We're at a relatively quiet spot on the promenade, and a bright-white beam of sunlight has just managed to break through the clouds overhead. "This was his spot…that's what he called it. *Sol's Spot*. I loved watching him swim. He looked so powerful out there, moving against the current. And he was always trying to get me to come play in the waves."

I glance at her. "You didn't swim?"

She shudders. "No way."

"Seriously?"

"Yeah. I have a fear of the ocean to be honest." Dani half-turns to look at me. "So…café lady."

"Shiran."

"Shi*ran*." Dani's tone is suggestive. "She met all the criteria, huh? Save for the fact that she's, you know. Not single."

I try to glare at her but end up laughing instead. "We didn't get to chat long enough before her Puma husband showed up. I'm not sure she was the nine-point woman."

"Nine points?" Dani straightens up. "Hang on. Do you have an actual *list*?"

"Of course I do." I'm amused by her amusement.

"Can I see it?"

"I guess." I pull the list out of my back pocket and hand it to her.

Dani laughs mockingly. "I'm sorry, you're just…carrying it around with you?"

"For luck," I say, feeling slightly defensive.

"Superstitious," Dani teases as she unfolds the paper. "Not very logical of you."

I watch as she skims the list quickly. "Well?"

"Two things," she says. "One…why is there a missing tenth point?"

I shrug. "When I started making it, I wanted ten points. But I couldn't think of the tenth, so…nine it is."

"Hmm." Dani nods seriously. "Okay. Two…do you think my relationship with Riley is doomed?"

I'm momentarily taken aback by the bluntness of her question. And I'm about to respond with a blunt "yes" of my own when I realise, she's joking.

"I haven't met Riley, so I wouldn't know," I say at last.

Dani chuckles. "Way to deflect. But here's the rundown: she's not Jewish, she's crazy tall, no one knows her natural hair colour but it's currently Ariel red, she—"

"Ariel?"

"The Little Mermaid kind of red?" Dani fluffs her auburn locks.

"Got it."

Dani glances at the list again. "She *is* good-looking, she's in this age bracket you've deemed more serious, *and* her career actually is taking off lately…her new boss has basically become like a mentor to her. She works late nearly every night and weekends."

I press my lips together, studying her face. Did I detect a hint of jealousy? But Dani moves on before I can decide.

"But starting with point seven, we are losing ground," she announces. "Stable family with no drama? Ha. Maybe sometime I'll tell you the story of how her aunt showed up to her sister's wedding wearing a full white lace *gown*."

Now I'm laughing. "Really?"

"Oh, that's just the beginning," Dani says. "Cake was thrown."

"Ouch."

"Point eight, wants to get married, point nine, wants children…" Dani's shoulders tense slightly and she falls silent.

"It's a no?" I ask gently.

Dani's quiet for so long, I start to regret asking. Then she says quietly, "It's not a no or a yes. It's an 'I haven't asked her, and we haven't talked about marriage.'"

I wince. "Ah."

Sighing, Dani hands the list back. "So? Do you deem us doomed?"

Yes. Obviously.

"Look, these are my criteria, not yours," I say, folding the paper up. "But if you really want my opinion…actually, scratch that. Facts matter, not opinions. And the fact is that statistics show long-distance relationships rarely work."

Dani sips her cup of coffee. "Well, it's a good thing I don't care about statistics," she says brightly. "Because I hate to break it to you, Bracha, but numbers have nothing to do with love. You love who you love, even when it doesn't make sense on paper."

"*You* might," I say. "I don't."

"*Im at omeret.*"

"If you say so." I'm inordinately pleased with myself for mentally translating. Then suddenly, I have an idea.

"One thing I did realise, thanks to Shiran, is that the perfect woman might not speak English flawlessly," I tell Dani. "And my Hebrew is, well…rusty. Do you know any tutors, programs, anything?"

"Sure, lots," Dani replies. "But the best way to brush up on a language is to have conversations." She flashes me a flirtatious smile. "Want a Hebrew partner?"

I can't help but lean a little closer. "I'd love that."

"Great!" Dani glances at her watch. "We can start right now if you'd care to escort me to work."

"I'd be delighted."

I'm surprised and a little pleased when she links her arm with mine. We stroll back up the promenade, chatting about the weather in Hebrew.

I like Dani. A lot, actually. But she's young and naive and I am 99.99 percent sure that this Riley is going to crush her spirit one day.

And that, I can't help but think, *is exactly why finding a wife should be a matter for the brain, not the heart.*

Chapter Seven

It turns out a lot of prospective perfect wives live in Tel Aviv.

I spend the weekend collecting phone numbers, and Sunday evening is devoted to organising them in order of potential and calling the top three to set up dates. First up is Yael, a raven-haired yoga master and cardiologist who I bumped into at a small grocery store while grabbing the dental floss I forgot to pack in my haste. Second is Hannah, the charming CEO of her own line of sportswear who happens to be one of Katya's massage clients. Third is Abigail, who Josh introduced me to at the hostel bar after his own attempt to make a pass at her failed.

"I'm sorry, Abby's *third*?" Josh stares at me in disbelief. We're in the kitchen Monday morning, and I'm pouring a cup of pregame coffee before my first date of the week. "Did you not hear me say she's a model? For Calvin Klein?"

"I heard you," I reply, taking a sip of coffee. "Three out of twelve is a good ranking, Josh."

"She's *an underwear model.*" Josh turns to Katya, who shrugs and offers a sweet smile.

"You're just mad my wingman game is stronger, Mr. Man Bun," she says. "Hannah's the one, Bracha. You'll see."

"Which one is this morning?" Josh asks. "More importantly, does she model underwear?"

"This morning is Yael, and no, she doesn't—at least, not yet." I wink at him.

What I don't tell Josh is that I'm not sure I fully trust his judgment on my ideal woman just yet. With looks and personality, yes. But when it comes to intelligence, I'm sceptical.

"I can't believe you picked that cafe again," Katya tells me. "Doesn't it feel like returning to the scene of the crime?"

I roll my eyes. "There was no *crime*."

"Adultery," Josh points out. "Well, almost."

"I didn't know Shiran was married," I say for probably the hundredth time. "And that's not the point. The Galya is a control in this dating experiment. It's the unchanging variable for every date. What if I took Yael to a terrible restaurant, then Hannah and I had a great lunch at another place? It might affect my judgment."

"Are you saying an exceptional hummus platter might lead to picking the wrong wife?" Katya deadpans, and Josh howls with laughter.

I fight back a smile. "It's a benchmark. Besides, Dani was right—the coffee there is great."

Despite Josh and Katya's teasing, I'm in high spirits when I enter The Galya. When I spot Yael at a table by the window, wearing a form-fitting cashmere sweater dress that hugs her incredibly toned frame, the whole debacle with Shiran and Puma man fades into a distant memory.

Over the next half hour, Yael and I talk shop. I tell her about Henry Roberts and his needle phobia. She counters with her own story about a teenage patient with an abnormally slow heartbeat who told all the kids at school that the new lump on his chest was not a pacemaker, but a spyware device installed by some shadowy member of the government.

"He swears his math teacher believes it," Yael tells me as I inch closer, "Says she's a total conspiracy theorist. All he has to do is tap his pacemaker and go kind of blank-eyed, like this…" She pauses, allowing her gaze to go unfocused. "And she gets all panicked. He's gotten out of three tests so far."

"Amazing." I smile feeling quite at home and relaxed in her eyes.

"His mum doesn't think so," Yael says with a warm smile. "Hey, do you have time for another coffee?"

"Absolutely," I reply, signalling to the barista. He gives the thumbs up, and I turn back to Yael. "So, you mentioned your sister's an anaesthesiologist. Were your parents doctors, too?"

Yael laughs. "Oh, no. Dad was in sales and Mum teaches piano. They were shocked when both their daughters ended up in medical school. Dad passes out if he so much as gets a paper cut."

A warm feeling envelops me as Yael continues talking about her family. *Eight points down, one to go,* I think. *If Yael wants kids, this contest might be over.*

The barista appears at our table with two steaming cups. "Here you go," he says, and I accept my black coffee with a thanks. But when he holds out the second cup to Yael, she leans back as if he's offering her a soaking wet rag.

"What is that?" Yael's voice has changed entirely. It's cold as ice and dripping with disdain. I stare at her, sure she must be making some sort of joke.

The barista blinks. "Cappuccino?"

Yael lets out a huffy sigh. "Not even close. I had the americano—with *skim* milk, no sugar."

"Alright," the barista murmurs, "I'll come back with that right away."

I sit up dead straight in shock as the barista hurries back to the counter and Yael shakes her head. "Honestly, do I look like I drink full-fat coffees?" She says, smoothing down her cashmere dress.

"You don't," I reply, standing up. Yael gives me a puzzled look as I head toward the counter. Glancing back at her, I pointedly drop a few shekels into tip jar near the register and loudly thank the barista before leaving the cafe.

When I get back to the hostel, my sour mood is lifted by the sight of Dani squatting in the corner of the lobby. She's facing the corner, and I walk up as quietly as possible.

"You know, there *are* restrooms in this place," I say, startling her.

"Ha ha." Straightening up, Dani swipes playfully at me with a yellow-tipped paintbrush. There's a speck of paint on her nose and I resist the urge to brush it off.

"Slow morning, plus I was feeling a little down, so I decided sunflowers were in order."

She nods at the corner and now I see a patch of

swirly yellow sunflowers have been added to the mural.

"Hang on," I say, gesturing around the lobby at large. "Did you paint this? I mean, *all* of this?"

Dani scratches her neck. "Depends. Do you think it's beautiful, or ugly?"

"I think it's…" I look around again, taking in the mural with renewed interest. The images are a curious mixture of hyper-realistic and abstract, vivid swirls of vaguely geometric shapes that form backgrounds only recognisable thanks to the overlaid intricate sketches painstakingly painted in the finest brush.

I realise Dani is watching me anxiously and I clear my throat.

"Bold," I say at last, and I mean it. "And dramatic. But not overly so."

Her face relaxes into a smile. "Really? You aren't just saying that?"

"Nah, I'd tell you if I thought it was rubbish."

Dani laughs. "High praise coming from you. I've never been more confident in my career path than I am right now."

For a second, I think she means working at the hostel reception desk. "You mean…a career as an artist?" I can't keep the surprise out of my voice.

Her smile falters slightly. "Yes, actually. You don't think I have the talent?"

"No, you're very talented," I say immediately. "It's just…what kind of career is art? Is there any money in it?"

Dani gives me a look that almost resembles

sympathy. "Oh, Bracha. Not all careers are about money."

"False," I retort. "All *jobs* are about money. They can also be about other things, but money is always part of the equation."

"I suppose so, but for me, it's a very, very small part," Dani says, looking around the lobby. "The primary reason I work here isn't because Omer pays well. It's because he lets me paint on the walls."

I follow her back to the reception desk, trying to wrap my head around what she's saying. *Murals don't pay the bills,* I want to say, but I don't because I don't think Dani would approve of my renewed Israeli bluntness.

Although I'm not sure why, I suddenly feel like I want her approval.

"Hey, wait a sec," she says suddenly, turning around. "Katya mentioned you had a date this morning. How was it? *Who* was it?"

I tilt my head back and sigh. "Yael. Gorgeous. Yogi. Cardiologist. Smart. Funny."

"Love is in the air," Dani says, but I hold up a finger to silence her.

"And," I add. "An absolute bitch to the barista."

Dani groans but she's grinning. "Well, that's a shame."

Several magazines are spread over the counter, most opened to dogeared pages. I begin smoothing down the pages and stacking them neatly in the right corner.

"Don't worry. Tomorrow, I'm meeting Hannah,

and Katya is positive she's the one," I tell Dani as I work. "I think it'll be more efficient if I prepare a list of questions. Something to help me quickly assess whether she has all nine points."

Dani shakes her head as she wipes off her paintbrush with a cloth. "This is crazy. I'm surprised you aren't collecting resumes."

"I would if that would speed the process up."

"Bracha, this isn't a job hunt!"

"No, it's not," I agree. "It's a wife hunt. Why wouldn't I take marriage as seriously as I take my career? Oh, speaking of—do you have time for a Hebrew lesson sometime today? Katya says Hannah's English is 'proficient' but I'm not sure what she means by that."

"Of course," Dani replies in perfectly joyful Hebrew. "How about right now?"

***

The barista looks amused when I walk into The Galya at five to ten the next morning.

"Another date?" he asks, already pulling the shots for my drink.

"Third time's a charm," I reply, and he laughs. His name is David, according to the tag pinned to his apron.

I'm just sitting down at what's officially become my usual table when an absolutely bombshell blonde strolls in. Even though some part of me knows this must be Hannah, thanks to Katya's flattering description, all I can see is Maddy. For a moment, guilt washes over me, and I'm tempted to text her again. But no—I sent three messages the day after our falling out. I just need to give her more time to cool down.

Instead, I focus on Hannah. She's exceptionally curvy, though I can't help but think she's getting a lot of assistance from the scrunched fabric on the butt of her bright blue leggings, not to mention her salmon pink vest, which is practically corseted—and pushes up her cleavage in a way that can't be conducive to a good workout.

"Double espresso, please," she says to David. I think of Yael's failed full-fat cappuccino and swallow a smile.

Hannah accepts her drink, then turns around and scans the cafe. I wave and her face lights up.

"Bracha?"

"That's me." I half-stand as she joins me, surprised but not displeased when she sets her drink down and gives me a full-on hug. Her thick, wavy hair smells like strawberries. When we pull apart, I switch to Hebrew. "Great to meet you."

She beams. "And you! Katya tells me you're from Sydney? I've always wanted to visit! What's it like? How's the beach?"

Or at least, that's what I think she says. Hannah speaks at lightning speed and I definitely didn't intend to launch us straight into a conversation entirely in Hebrew. But my pride won't allow me to beg for mercy and switch back to English, so I keep up as best I can.

Ten minutes in, I'm thinking I need to send Dani a thank-you card. Practicing with her must have helped more than I realised because I'm holding my own with this beautiful motor-mouth. That is, until Hannah decides to get a snack. She calls to David and orders a chocolate muffin.

"Would you like one?" she asks.

"No thanks."

"Are you sure?"

"I am sure."

Hannah freezes, her blue eyes wide. David also does a double take and I even notice an older man reading the newspaper at a nearby table glance up.

"Excuse me?" Hannah's voice has gone high-pitched.

I frown. "*Ani btulh*," I repeat in slow, clear Hebrew.

I know it's correct. I used this phrase a few times yesterday with Dani. But obviously, something has gone wrong.

"Really?" Hannah squeaks.

I'm starting to get frustrated. "*Ani btulh*," I insist. "I am sure!" I say in English this time.

"Okay, I believe you!" Hannah sounds almost alarmed. "And that's…cool? I mean, it's nothing to be ashamed of! I'm just not sure why you're bringing it up now."

David snaps his fingers. "Oh, I see," he says in English, giving me an almost apologetic look. "I believe she meant to say, *I am sure. Ani btucha.*"

"Oh." Hannah's shoulders slump. Then she claps

her hands over her mouth. "Oh, *oh!*"

And she starts to laugh uncontrollably.

"*Ani btucha,*" I say to David, trying to hide my irritation. "What did I say?"

"*Ani btulh,*" David replies awkwardly.

"What does that mean?"

The older man at the next table clears his throat. "It means 'I am a virgin,'" he says in thickly accented English and Hannah's giggles turn to outright howls of laughter.

My face burns hot, and I try to wave it off. By the time David brings Hannah her muffin, she's hiccupping loudly, her cheeks red from laughter.

"Thank you," she manages to choke out.

"Can I get you anything else?" he asks.

"No thanks," Hannah says, her eyes sparkling. "I am a virgin."

As she bursts into fresh peals of laughter, I force a smile at David, stand up, mutter, "Check, please," and leave Hannah to revel in what will undoubtedly be the highlight of her day.

***

Back at the hostel, I head straight to the bar. After the forty-five minutes of teasing I just endured, I think I've earned a drink. I spot Katya and Josh at a table in the far corner and head toward them, fully intending to tell Katya exactly what I thought about Hannah. But then Katya stands, tugging Josh's hand with a coy look and he happily allows himself to be pulled out of the bar and, I'm guessing, to Katya's room.

Sighing, I reverse course and head to the lobby instead. Josh and Katya have been all over each other ever since my first night here. It's cute but also a tad bit annoying. After all, they must know it'll just end in disaster.

Dani is reading a novel behind the reception desk, her feet propped up on the counter. The magazines are in disarray again—one has even fallen on the floor. I march up and swat her ballet flats, causing her to yelp.

"What was that for?"

"For your little prank," I say as I angrily stack the magazines. "Teaching me the wrong phrase."

Her brow furrows. "What phrase?"

"You know what phrase."

"I do?"

"I'm *sure* you do." I put an emphasis on *sure*. But Dani looks as confused as ever. "Fine, don't admit it then."

"Bracha, I don't know what you're talking about."

"*Ani btucha.*" I pause. "You taught me to say *ani btulh.*"

Dani's mouth falls open. "I most certainly did not! *Ani btucha*—you were saying it perfectly yesterday."

I believe her. And that makes my mood even worse. Because what I'm looking for right now is a scapegoat, but I've got no one to blame but myself.

"So," Dani presses her lips together, her eyes dancing with amusement. "I take it wife interview number three didn't go well?"

Without responding, I turn on heel and head to my room.

"I'm sure number four will be better!" Dani calls after me. "But maybe don't tell her you're a virgin until the second date!"

***

Josh was right. I should have ranked the underwear model at the top of the list.

Abby is sweet and graceful, with porcelain skin and delicate features. She's already at The Galya when I walk in and I instantly give her a bonus point for punctuality. When I order a black coffee, she says, "make that two."

"Coming right up." David winks at me before turning away.

It doesn't take long before I realise I never should have doubted Josh. Abby is quick to tell me that her modelling jobs pay for graduate school. She's currently earning her doctorate in pharmacology, with plans to work in the clinical research field. I feel guilty when I realise she's probably always quick to bring this up on dates with women like me who mistakenly assume that models are airheads.

"There's a trial for a new drug that could potentially treat COPD starting next year that I'm hoping to work on," she tells me. "My father and grandmother both suffered from emphysema, so it's a particular passion of mine."

"That sounds incredible." *And so are you,* I can't help but think. Abby is ticking all the points, one by one.

"So, what made you decide to work in an ED?" Abby asks with a smile. "Adrenaline junkie?"

I laugh. "I actually started in—"

"*I wanna milkshaaaaaaaaake!*"

Abby and I turn in time to see a toddler in a bright green dress throw herself onto the tiled floor in front of the register, wailing at the top of her lungs. Her mother, a young woman in sweatpants and an oversized cardigan, is unfazed by her child's cries.

"Lily, sweetie, they don't make milkshakes here, but how about a chocolate milk?" She says calmly.

"Kids hey," I say, turning back to Abby.

Her face is a mask of disdain. "Are they supposed to be cute?"

I'm taken aback by the disgust in her tone. "Well, yes, sometimes."

Abby shakes her head. "Parents should know better than to take children that young out to places like this." The little girl's sobs increase in volume and Abby's nostrils flare. She raises her voice to an almost shout. "It's inconsiderate to customers who paid good money for coffee in a relatively peaceful environment."

The mother turns around to face Abby and gives her a sharp look.

"If my baby is bothering you, maybe you should go somewhere else."

Abby opens her mouth to respond but the mother

cuts her off, her voice firm and unapologetic, "I don't need you to tell me how to handle my daughter, seeing as you clearly have no children of your own."

The little girl's sobs grow louder, but the mother remains calm, still trying to comfort her. She turns back to David, who hands her the to-go cup, and without a second glance at Abby, she pays and starts to walk toward the door, dragging her still-screaming toddler behind her.

Abby watches them leave, her face tight with annoyance.

"Well, that was uncomfortable," Abby mutters with an exaggerated shutter. "That sound was like fingernails on a chalkboard and all over a milkshake. Have you ever seen such a brat?"

I stare at her perfect porcelain doll face. "No," I say truthfully. "I haven't."

***

When I walk into the hostel lobby, Omer places his hand over his heart.

"My poor Bracha," he says. "You look as if you have been punched in the stomach."

"Close. I just saw an underwear model punch a toddler. And her mother. Not literally," I add hastily seeing Omer's look of horror. "Just…bad date, that's all."

"I'm sorry to hear that," Omer says, reaching over the desk to offer me a cigarette. "What happened?"

Before I can wave my hand in a 'No' fashion to

Omer, Dani bursts out of the office, waving her phone over her head.

"Guess what guess what guess what!" She cries, twirling in circles like a little girl playing ballerina.

Omer claps his hands in delight. "She's finally coming?"

"She's finally coming!" Dani pulls Omer into an impromptu jig and he happily obliges. When Dani notices me, she tries to pull me around the desk to join them in their rendition of the Horah.

I step back. "I'm good, thanks. Who's coming?"

"Riley!" Dani says breathlessly, falling still. Her auburn curls fall loose over her shoulders and her cheeks are flushed with happiness.

"She'll be here for Silvester, I mean New Year's Eve, I mean Novi God. Ah, you know what I mean, Bracha?!" Dani practically sings at me in Hebrew, and I'm too annoyed to appreciate how smooth and rhythmic her Hebrew sounds.

"I really didn't think it was going to happen—her boss has been so annoying lately."

"Well, not everyone can be a boss like me," Omer says, winking as he heads into the office out of breath and in a sweat.

"Would her boss really make everyone work on New Year's Eve?" I ask, bending down to pick up a magazine face down on the floor.

Dani makes a face and slowly unwinds from her jig. "Not everyone. Just Riley. It's like this woman thinks Riley is her personal assistant. She keeps demanding Riley come with her on all these business trips. One was during American Thanksgiving! We thought she'd get a week off to come see me but no, she got dragged to some conference in Atlantic City."

She keeps talking, and I keep listening, straightening up the magazines. So Dani's girlfriend has been going on trips with her female boss…including a trip to Atlantic City for a supposed conference. One held during a national holiday, no less.

I glance at Dani, and a tiny ache forms in my chest. Because I have a feeling a few minutes of Googling would reveal there was no business conference in Atlantic City over the Thanksgiving holiday.

And I can't help but wonder if Riley's boss might end up taking her on another cosy trip over New Year's Eve.

Chapter Eight

As the week passes, I double my efforts—and my caffeine intake. But it seems like every woman I meet has one fatal flaw that takes them out of the running.

Wednesday afternoon, I have coffee with Sarah, a friend of Katya's cousin. Her drink: iced black tea. Her flaw: she recently quit her job at a law firm to sell essential oils. It took about five minutes for me to realise that she was less interested in dating me and more interested in roping me into her pyramid scheme.

Thursday morning sees me with Ruth, a chiropractor who treated Josh a few times. Her drink: Nescafe instant. Her flaw: she ends up in a FaceTime argument with her sister over a missing necklace that ends in her screaming, "Do I look like I have it?!" while tugging down the neckline of her blouse as everyone in the cafe stares.

That afternoon, I'm back at The Galya with Jean, Omer's neighbour. Her drink: double espresso with a shot of caramel. Her flaw: upon learning where I'm from, she spends the better part of an hour telling me about her Aussie ex, who is a "possessive psychopath" whose evening tea Jean would dose with laxatives so she could sneak out to meet her friends, leaving me with little doubt as to who the real psychopath is.

The punishment continues Friday morning with Maya, who met Katya and Josh at a club. Her drink:

black coffee spiked with her own heavy-handed shot of whiskey. Her flaw: she was a trust fund kid whose gap year had turned into a gap decade.

"See you later this afternoon?" David asks when I drop a few more shekels in the tip jar on my way out. I heave a sigh and nod and he chuckles.

But the truth is, I haven't even called the next woman—Rose, or was it Rosi? —yet. I never thought I'd say this but I'm feeling a little burned out on dating.

Back at the hostel, Dani is at the desk chatting with a redheaded woman with an unmistakable Californian accent who is wearing a slouchy blue beanie. For a moment, I think Riley's arrived early and I experience an unwelcome and confusing mix of irritation and jealousy.

"Bracha, over here!" Dani calls with a bright smile. The other woman turns and I realise she can't be more than twenty-two. So, this isn't Riley.

"Hi there," the woman says, looking me up and down in a brazen way I can't help but admire. "I've heard a lot about you in the last ten minutes!"

"Oh?" I look at Dani questioningly.

"This is Rachel," Dani explains. "I was checking her in and we got to chatting. She's here on her Birthright trip."

"Nice," I say, offering Rachel a half-hearted smile. "So, you just arrived today?"

"That's right," Rachel replies. "Although, like I was telling Dani, it was all kind of last minute. My girlfriend of almost two years dumped me a few weeks ago and I was like, 'why am I even in San Diego?' I mean, I only stayed there after college because of her job. Before I knew it, I was booking a flight to Tel Aviv to join my friends on this trip!"

Dani winks at me. "You aren't the only spontaneous single lady here. I thought you two might hit it off!" Reaching beneath the counter, she whips out two bright yellow slips of paper. "Besides, Rachel here is our tenth check-in today, which means she wins these free coffee vouchers!"

"Ooh!" Rachel grabs the vouchers, clearly delighted.

At last it dawns on me that Dani is trying to play wingman. I open my mouth to make some excuse, fully intending to head back to my room for some quiet time to recover from yet another disastrous date.

"Just let me freshen up, and I'll meet you right back here in a few!" Rachel's fingers graze my arm and she smiles before grabbing her bag and heading down the hall.

Heaving a sigh, I turn to find Dani beaming at me. "Cute, right?"

"Cute," I agree. "And so, *so* young."

"She's almost twenty-three."

"Young." I rub my eyes, suddenly exhausted. "I appreciate the help, but she doesn't exactly match my criteria, aside from the physical. She's here for ten days. She just got dumped. She's here to hook up with strangers, not start a long-term relationship."

"You don't know that for sure," Dani says. "She said her girlfriend dumped her when she turned thirty.

She's into older women, Bracha."

I make a face. "I take offense at the implication that I'm an older woman."

"Take offense all you like, you are nearly thirty." Dani smiles sweetly. "Come on, just give her a shot! Isn't this why you're here?"

I hate to admit it, but she's right. "Sometimes you have to fail a heap of interviews before landing your dream job," I say.

"Save the sweet talk for her," Dani teases, and I laugh.

Half an hour later, Rachel and I are sipping our free coffees at a table in the hostel bar. I let Rachel do most of the talking, and she happily obliges, rattling on about her degree in media communications, her growing TikTok following, and her plans to start her own consulting business for influencers trying to build their social media presence.

"I have so many posts planned for this trip," Rachel tells me, tugging at her beanie. "The street art in Florentin, that Ben-Gurion statue on the beach, Habima Square…wow, New Year's Eve alone will give me enough content for a week!"

That gets my attention. "You're going to be here for New Year's? Birthright trips are only for ten days, aren't they?"

"Oh, right." Rachel smirks a little. "My flight home is next week. But there's no freaking way I'm going back to Cali for the holidays."

"Because of your ex?"

Rachel shakes her head. "Because of my family.

Omigod, they're such a nightmare. My sister just had a baby and it's just heteronormative hell with them around, you know? My mum and dad are *so* into the grandparent thing—my mum actually started baking? Like, hello, would've been nice if she knew how to turn on the oven when I was little, but whatever. My sister and her husband actually threw a gender reveal party last summer. The whole thing where they cut the cake and it's either pink or blue, you know? My sister asked me to pick it up, and when I did, I asked the guy at the bakery, and he said it was blue inside. When I walked in, I was like, congrats! You're having a Smurf! Everyone got mad at me because they took it so freaking seriously, saying I ruined the surprise—"

A distant buzzing noise fills my ears, mercifully drowning Rachel out as she continues talking shit about her family. The longer I sat there, the more irritated I felt.

Dani, I decide firmly, is no wingman. For that matter, neither are Omer or Josh or Katya. In fact, I'm done with amateur wingmen hooking me up with women who aren't *it*.

I'm done with wingmen, period. The only person who can find my perfect wife is me.

***

I finally manage to ditch Rachel with an excuse about needing to call my father. When I return to the lobby, Josh is at the front desk chatting with Dani.

"Where's Katya?" I ask, joining them. "Finally get

sick of one another?"

It comes out harsher than I intended.

"She's massaging Omer. Keeps saying she's saving up for that ticket to India but I think she's all talk about that trip." Josh squints at me. "You okay?"

"Not really. Bad date." I give Dani a pointed glare. "And seriously, what is with these magazines?" I add bending over to pick up two that are on the floor. "Is it that hard to keep things organised?"

Dani looks like she's trying not to laugh, which only irritates me further. "What was wrong with Rachel?"

"Exactly what I told you from the start," I retort. "She's *young*. Immature. Know what her grand career plans are? Building a following on TikTok by telling people how to build a following on TikTok. That's like becoming a bestselling author by publishing a book telling people how to become a bestselling author. Making a living out of telling people how to do something you haven't even done yourself? It's the dumbest thing I've ever heard."

"Tell that to all the hedge fund bros making millions telling other people what to do with their money," Josh says drily.

I ignore this and focus on Dani. "Thanks to you, I'm going to have to figure out how to avoid this girl for the next month!"

Dani frowns. "Birthright trips are only ten days."

"She's staying through New Year's because apparently spending the holidays with her family is, what'd she call it?" I pause, pretending to think. "Oh, right—heteronormative hell. Although if you ask me, they'll have a better time without her. She ruined her sister's gender reveal baby shower on purpose."

"To be fair, gender reveal parties are incredibly dumb," Josh points out.

"Not the point." I rub my temples. "It's just so immature. And so *mean*. God, this week has been a never-ending series of crappy dates."

Dani pats my arm sympathetically. "Well, I'm sorry Rachel wasn't the one. But bad dates are part of the journey, right? It's helping you discover what you want in a partner."

Something in her tone really rubs me the wrong way.

"I already know what I want in a partner," I say angrily. "I have a list. The problem is that I haven't been sticking to it."

"Or maybe," Dani muses, "The list *is* the problem."

"Maybe shitty wingmen are the problem," I snap back.

Dani arches an eyebrow. "Maybe trying to find a partner based on cold hard facts rather than looking for actual *love* is the problem."

"Maybe—"

"Okay!" Josh cuts in, moving between us like a referee. "How about we all just take a breath?"

"Good idea." Turning, I head for the doors.

Outside, a cold breeze slaps me right in the face. I take a few steps down the street, then lean against the wall and sigh. I'm so tired. I've lost all motivation. And if I'm being honest, I'm getting a little sick of Tel Aviv and the weather.

"Hey."

I glance up as Josh joins me. "Sorry," I mumble. "I didn't mean to drag you into that."

"No worries," Josh says, leaning against the wall next to me. "And for what it's worth, Dani was just trying to help."

I let out a noncommittal grunt. For a few minutes, we stand there in silence.

"Bracha," Josh says finally. "Can I make an observation?"

"Sure."

He turns to face me. "I get that this whole 'find a wife' thing is really important to you. But you're taking this search way too seriously."

"Marriage should be taken seriously," I point out.

"Yeah, but I mean…finding that person should be enjoyable, you know?" Josh's eyes flick back to the hostel entrance. "I mean, you're on holiday, you're going on tonnes of dates…this is the fun part."

"It'd be a lot more fun if the dates actually fit my criteria," I say. "Instead, I've got Dani setting me up with a literal child. Or you setting me up with a woman who hates children. I appreciate the help and all, but wasting my time is *not* fun, Josh. And all Dani's waffle about journeys is exactly that—wasting time. Which is exactly what she's doing with her so-called girlfriend, by the way. I'm not about to take relationship advice from someone whose partner is clearly having an affair."

Josh sticks his hands in his pockets. "Dani really got to you, huh?"

There's a playful hint in his words that I choose to ignore. "No. She's just oblivious. And I—" I close my eyes and rest my head against the wall. "I'm wondering if I made a mistake coming here at all."

Josh nudges my arm. "What about what your mom wanted for you?" he asks softly.

At the mention of mum, my throat tightens. Mum wanted me to be happy and right now, I'm a far cry from happy. I picture myself in our warm, cosy kitchen, sitting at the table slicing bread while Mum serves up two bowls of her potato leek soup.

Then I picture her setting out a third bowl and my eyes fly open.

"Shit," I mutter, pulling my phone out of my pocket and staring at the date on the screen. "*Shit.*"

"What's wrong?" Josh asks.

What's wrong is that Eli was released from prison yesterday. My convicted felon brother could be sitting at my kitchen table in my house right this second and I've been so busy drowning in terrible dates that I'd nearly forgotten.

My pulse begins to race. Maybe he's moved into his old room. Maybe he's calling realtors. That house is supposed to be the home for my future family and here I am halfway around the world.

"I need to make a call," I tell Josh. He waves as I head down to the end of the block.

I duck down a quiet alley, my heartbeat thrumming in my ears. Opening my contacts, I find

Dad's number, brace myself, and hit *call*.

It rings nearly six times before he picks up. "Bracha? What's wrong?"

He sounds alarmed and his voice is thick with sleep. With a surge of guilt, I realise it's the middle of the night for him.

"Ah, sorry," I say quickly. "Nothing's wrong. I forgot the time change."

"Time change?" Dad pauses. "Bracha, where are you? And why haven't you replied to my texts? I've been worried!"

Shit shit shit. I'm already regretting making this call.

"Sorry," I repeat. "I decided to take a…holiday. Last minute kind of thing. To, um…to Tel Aviv."

"Really?" Now Dad sounds fully awake. "That's great! Very unlike you."

The relief in his voice only compounds my guilt. "Yeah, it was pretty spontaneous. Listen, I only just realised that yesterday was…that Eli, you know…and I was wondering where he is."

"Ah." Dad clears his throat. "Right, yes. I picked him up yesterday afternoon. He's staying with me for now."

I pull my phone away from my ear and stare at it. "He's what?"

"Just until he gets on his feet," Dad says quickly. "It can be difficult for people who served time to find work, so I'm——"

"Hey, Dad?" I cut in loudly. "Sorry, but I've got to run, okay? Call you later."

I hang up, my phone shaking in my hand. I don't

want to hear about Dad talk about poor Eli's struggles. He's not going to get any sympathy from me. After everything Eli did, everything he put Mum through, how can Dad even think about supporting him now?

Josh is sitting with his back to the wall when I return a few minutes later, playing a game on his phone. It's only now that I notice the dusty old backpack sitting at his feet.

"Going somewhere?" I ask, sitting next to him.

He lowers his phone and gives me a sheepish look. "Yeah, actually. I let Katya talk me into getting out of the city for a weekend."

"Really?" It's my turn to elbow him now. "Romantic couple's getaway to a bed and breakfast, huh? Things are getting serious. Next thing you know, she'll be dragging you off to India."

"Fat chance." Josh snorts. "As for the kibbutz, digging around in the dirt is hardly my idea of a romantic getaway but Katya loves the whole farm experience, so."

"Huh." I picture my childhood diary, a smile playing on my lips. "I lived on a kibbutz once when I was a teenager. Met a girl."

"Oh yeah?"

"Yeah. Naomi." I pause. "You'd be surprised how romantic a kibbutz can be, actually."

"I'll believe it when I see it," Josh says. "Hey, why don't you come?"

I wrinkle my nose. "Look, I like you and Katya a lot, but I'm not interested in—"

"Oh, shut up." Josh shoves my shoulder. "I'm serious. You met a girl at a kibbutz once, right? Maybe it'll happen again. And no offense but you seem pretty beat down right now. If anything, getting out of the city might help clear your head."

I have every intention of declining. But then I remember the words scrawled in my diary. *Her breath smells like mint and her hair smells like coconuts. She has a little mole over her mouth, just like Drew Barrymore. Her laugh is kind of mellow and it literally makes my legs turn into mush.*

And I remember the first time Naomi kissed me. The way she'd been laughing, then her eyes looked deep into mine in a way that made me realise what was about to happen. The way I thought my heart might beat right out of my chest as she moved closer and closer until our lips pressed together, and it felt like some part of me, I didn't even know existed, opened up and our bodies pressed together.

I want that again. That feeling of experiencing something new and exciting. And maybe Josh is right. Maybe I've been looking for it in the wrong place.

"Give me fifteen minutes to pack," I tell him, and he lets out a whoop as I race back inside.

Chapter Nine

Katya's free spirit and spontaneous behaviour make her a fun clubbing partner. But I'd rather spend all day trying to untangle headphones than let her handle my travel plans ever again.

The trip takes over three hours and involves four bus transfers and hitchhiking along a highway. By the time we arrive, the stars are out in full, dazzling array in the night sky. We're greeted by a friendly bearded man named Gideon who shows us to the small, three-room home with basic accommodations we'll be staying in for the weekend. After a rather sleepless night, thanks to the thin walls and Josh and Katya's boisterous activities, I'm roused at dawn to start the workday.

By noon, with my favourite jeans covered in mud and my nails caked with dirt, I've come to understand the truth of my situation. I've just voluntarily left the bright lights and conveniences of Tel Aviv to pick potatoes on a farm that is, from what I can tell, completely devoid of lesbians.

Around noon, I wearily head to the open-plan lounge surrounded by mango trees where several workers have already congregated. I sit alone under the tin roof, enjoying the relief from the bitter wind. Garlic hangs from every corner of the lounge's wooden beams. Presumably, it's there to ward off snakes or the body odour; I can't be sure which. The kitchen is next door—I checked the fridge this morning, and it contained only coffee and milk. You pick your own food at Summer Fields, and you cook it too, or you don't eat.

"Hey, Bracha!" Josh strolls up, carrying a massive sack of carrots on one shoulder. I haven't spotted another carrot picker yet; from the looks of it, Josh dug them all up himself.

"Are you always the first to finish?" I ask.

"Depends on the girl."

"Hilarious."

Josh whistles cheerily as he drops the sack. I watch him, amused despite my exhaustion. I didn't think Josh would take to the kibbutz life so quickly, but I suppose his good mood has much more to do with the activities he and Katya got up to last night while I attempted to sleep.

"Look at that!" Katya appears, carrying her own much smaller sack of carrots. She's one of those women who glows when she sweats and who wears a little dirt and grunge in an appealing, hippie Mother Nature kind of way. She drops her morning bounty next to Josh's and gives him a kiss on the cheek. "You must have twenty kilos at least!"

"Carrot soup's on for tonight!" Josh replies. "And tomorrow night. And the night after."

"With some delicious roasted potatoes," Katya adds, nudging my sack with her toe. "Morning, Brachaleh."

"Afternoon," I say pointedly. "What are you doing?"

She crouches next to me, holding out her phone and squishing her face next to mine. I barely have time to register that she's taking a selfie, and my smile looks more like a grimace.

"Beautiful!" Katya declares. "I'm definitely sharing that one."

"Are you getting reception out here?" I ask. "Because my phone has been showing zero bars all morning."

"There's a magic spot by those cactus bushes," Katya says, snaking her arm around Josh's neck and pressing their cheeks together. They kiss as she snaps another photo and when it becomes clear neither are coming up for air anytime soon, I wander over to the cacti.

"Oh, come on," I murmur when two bars appear on my phone screen. My battery is at twenty-three percent thanks to not one but two power outages last night, so I set it to low power mode.

I spend a few much-needed minutes texting back and forth with Leo who thinks it's hilarious that I've left the second-most populous city in Israel to spend the weekend on a remote southern farm with a few dozen heteros.

Turning a straight farmer gay sounds like a fun challenge, but maybe not when you're on a deadline!

His jokes cheer me up a little, but the truth is, coming here has only compounded my loneliness. It doesn't help that Josh and Katya are so deliriously happy.

But if I thought I was at rock bottom, I was

wrong. That came when I opened Instagram and saw my own sweaty, haggard face smooshed against Katya's glowing cheek. The top comment was from Dani: *"Adorable! Have a great weekend!"*

Naturally, I check out her account and that's when I see her most recent photo, featuring her wrapped around a red-haired Amazon like a kitten climbing a tree trunk.

Apparently, Riley had made it to Tel Aviv after all.

When my phone vibrates, I nearly drop it. I accept the call, trying not to think about Dani and her irritatingly hot girlfriend.

"Leo?"

"Yeah."

At the sound of Leo's voice, a wave of homesickness nearly knocks me to my knees. Pressing my hand to my stomach, I close my eyes and try to keep the despair out of my voice.

"What's up?"

"I'm surprised you were even able to text." Leo's voice is uncharacteristically tight. "I figured your reception would be crap."

"It is. I'm practically sitting on a cactus because apparently this is the only spot on the kibbutz that gets a signal."

"Magic cactus."

"Yeah." I pause. "Leo, what's wrong?"

"What makes you think something's wrong?"

"Texts are for jokes. Calls are for emergencies."

He sighs. "Fine. So…Eli was just here."

My shiver runs over my back, and I start to sit

down before remembering I'm standing in front of a damned cactus. "Fuck," I whisper. "What'd he do?"

"Not much," Leo admitted. "Just kind of walked around, inspected the place. Pointed out that mould on the ceiling in the bathroom—"

"I've got someone coming to fix that!"

"And he fixed that leaky sink in the upstairs bathroom." Leo paused. "He went through some of your Mum's stuff, too."

I squeeze my hand into a fist, digging my nails into my palm. "Did he take anything?"

"No."

Aunt Aggie pipes up in the background. "He was very civil, Brachaleh! He even had a haircut. Looked nice. Presentable."

"Oh, well that makes everything better," I say sarcastically. "Look, Leo, I need you to…to do something."

Leo sighs. "I'm not sure there's anything I *can* do."

"Change the locks," I tell him. "Call a locksmith. I'm serious."

"Bracha, it's his mother's house too. I can't—"

"Leo, please." My voice is shaking. "Just until I get back, okay? Then I'll deal with him." I pause, but Leo says nothing. "Leo? Hello?"

I glance at my screen to see if we were disconnected, then let out a loud curse when I see the dim red *no battery* sign. My phone is officially dead.

Closing my eyes, I take a few deep breaths. Powerless. That's exactly how I feel right now.

The last time I saw Eli in Mum's house was a week

before his arrest. He'd had a massive argument with Mum, one that left her in bed for days, barely eating, crying when she thought I couldn't hear her.

Is that what he was thinking about when he was digging through her things? Does he have even a shred of guilt over what he did to her?

Of course he doesn't. He's Eli. He only thinks about himself.

"Bracha?" Josh calls. "Want some lunch?"

Steeling myself, I head back to my friends. I don't want lunch. I want working electricity, a hot shower and maybe a good massage. I want my mum. I want to get Eli the hell out of my house. I want to get back to Tel Aviv. But right now, I'll have to settle for carrot soup.

Chapter Ten

Picking potatoes all weekend under the desert sun had one benefit: I arrived back at the hostel with a better tan in the dead of winter.

"Sorry it was a failure, wife-wise," Katya says, adjusting her backpack straps as we cross the street leaving the bus station. "But hey, I can make it up to you."

"It's not your fault you picked a lesbian-free kibbutz," I tell her without taking my eyes off the hostel. I can't quite make out who's in the lobby through the glass doors. Is Dani working? More importantly, is Riley with her? For some reason, the thought of Riley hanging around while Dani manages the front desk irritates me.

"Technically, it wasn't lesbian-free," Katya points out. "You were there. But I one hundred percent guarantee this Novi God party at Club Who will be…what's the opposite of lesbian free?"

Josh grins. "Lesbian stocked? Piled high with lesbians? Lesbian packed?"

"That. Thank you, Mr. Man Bun." Katya glances at me. "Bracha, are you even listening?"

"I heard you." My pulse quickens as I pull open the door. "Piles of lesbians at Club Who. Man Bun. Sounds great."

Dani looks up as we enter, and our eyes meet. In that moment, two things dawn on me simultaneously.

First, I missed her. I'm not an idiot. Logically, I know Dani is not in the running when it comes to my search for the perfect wife. She's young, she's flighty, and most importantly—she's taken. But in the few weeks I've been here, we've become friends. I like her.

Which is why the second thing I notice causes my heart to twist.

She's been crying.

"Hey, guys!" Dani smiles brightly, but her eyes are red-rimmed, and her nose is pink. "Welcome back! How was the kibbutz?"

"*We* had a great time," Josh says, slipping his arm around Katya and pulling her close. "Bracha, not so much."

"What are you talking about?" I say sarcastically. "Digging potatoes out of the dirt, sleeping on a hard cot, no hot water for showers, absolutely zero gay women…now that's my idea of a good time."

Dani laughs. "Well, I'm glad you're back," she tells me, and something in her tone grips my stomach.

"Me too," I reply.

"You're tan." Dani says softly.

"Kind of." I examine my arms.

"Must be your skin tone."

"Well, my dad was dark and hairy."

Dani tilts her head. "I can see that." She studies my arms closely and I feel heat rush up my neck.

I go to respond but fall short of words as I realise Dani is looking at me in a way I haven't seen before.

Katya clears her throat. "Well, we're going to get cleaned up," she says, tugging Josh's hand. "Meet you at the bar later, Bracha?"

"Sounds good."

The moment Josh and Katya disappear down the hall, I look at Dani. "So, what happened?"

"What do you mean?"

"You've been crying."

"Oh." Dani wipes her eyes, even though they're dry. "Klum." She says in Hebrew.

"It's clearly not nothing."

Dani sighs. "Fine. Riley called this morning. She's not coming."

"Isn't she already here?" I blurt out, then mentally curse myself.

"No." Dani frowns. "Why?"

I cast around for a non-embarrassing explanation. When I find none, I'm forced to admit the truth. "I saw that photo you posted of the two of you."

"Ah, that." Dani shakes her head. "It's from the last time we saw each other. I posted it a few days ago because…I had a feeling she wasn't coming, and I guess I was trying to guilt her. Which is really shitty of me."

"It's shitty of her to ditch you for her boss," I point out.

Dani arches a brow. "I didn't say that's why she bailed."

"But it is, isn't it?"

"Yes," Dani admits. "Work trip. This time to Las Vegas."

For a New Year's Eve business conference? I can't help but think. I want to tell Dani to open her eyes, to

108

acknowledge the reality: Riley is almost certainly having an affair with her boss. But I don't want to push her away and, right now, we're close.

Physically, I mean. She's leaning over the counter, chin in her hands and her face is close enough for me to find constellations in her freckles. Which are insanely gorgeous.

"So now I've got no plans for tomorrow night." Dani taps a finger on her cheek, her gaze locked onto mine. "No one to bring in the new year with. No one to kiss at midnight. What's a girl to do?"

"Hmm." I play along, pretending to think about it. Then I snap my fingers. "Hey, why don't you come to Club Who with us? Katya swears their Novi God party is the best in Tel Aviv. A few shots of vodka will probably help you feel better."

"Maybe a few dozen shots," Dani says with a wry smile. "So…are you asking me to spend New Year's Eve with you, Bracha?"

"Yes." I pause. "With me, Josh and Katya. And, you know, a few hundred other people."

For a fraction of a second, Dani leans in, closing the distance between us until our lips are little more than a breath apart. Her perfume is warm and intoxicating and all I want is to get even closer. Then she straightens up and I exhale sharply, feeling a strange mix of disappointment and relief.

"Sure," she says smoothly. "But you'd better be ready to show me a good time, Bracha Cohen."

She winks before heading back into the office. I watch her go, feeling a mix of frustration and anticipation, thinking tomorrow night can't come soon enough.

***

According to Katya, Club Who won't even let us in unless we're wearing blue and white.

"The crazier the outfit, the better," she'd added. "Which means you and I have a little shopping to do, Bracha."

Quarter to nine on New Year's Eve finds me standing in front of the slightly warped mirror in my hostel room wearing a bright blue jumpsuit with flared legs. The narrow neckline cuts down to my navel. It's not my usual style, but when Katya spotted it, she ordered me to try it on. With my hair swooped over in a sharp side part and my collarbones sparkling with Katya's body glitter, I have to admit I look pretty hot.

Though I try not to acknowledge it, a small part of me hopes Dani thinks so, too.

As if on cue, my phone buzzes. Dani's sent a selfie in a wig with wild, electric blue layers that perfectly frame her face. *Crazy enough?*

I grin as I reply with a thumbs up. A moment later, she responds with the kiss emoji.

With a fresh surge of adrenaline, I pocket my phone and head to the lobby where Katya and Josh are waiting. She's worked her magic on him—I have to admit, the white tuxedo with no shirt look should be cheesy, but Josh makes it work. Katya looks even more stunning than usual in a flowing white dress with dozens of tiny blue flowers pinned to her long curls.

Josh lets out a wolf whistle when he sees me. "Now that's a *look*," he says approvingly.

Katya presses her hand to her chest. "Bracha, tonight's the night you dance with your future wife. I can feel it."

I smile and follow them to the doors but secretly, I'm thinking I might want to put the wife search on hold tonight. There's only one person I want to dance with at this party.

Midnight is over two hours away, but Club Who is already raging. Blacklights swirl and flash around the dance floor and given that everyone is wearing blue and white, it creates a bombastic, almost ethereal look, like hundreds of gyrating aliens moving in time to the infectious beat of Pink's "Raise Your Glass."

Katya vanishes into the crowd, reappearing moments later with three fizzy, electric blue cocktails.

"How'd you get those so fast?" Josh exclaims, glancing over at the swarmed bar.

Katya gives him a coy smile as she clinks her glass first to his, then to mine. "What can I say? I caught the bartender's eye."

Katya and Josh down the cocktails as if they're shots, then hit the dance floor. I sip mine as I keep to the outskirts, scanning the crowd. The cocktail is good—chilled vodka with blue Curacao and tonic—but I need to take it slow. I want to keep my wits about me until I find Dani.

The problem is the sheer number of blue wigs. I glance at my phone, wondering if I should text her.

Maybe a cheeky *so what are you wearing?*

Wincing, I put my phone back in my pocket without texting. What am I doing? Yes, Dani's girlfriend is almost certainly cheating on her. She's definitely taking Dani for granted, constantly cancelling trips and making empty promises, but that doesn't change the fact that Dani is in a relationship.

Are they monogamous? It occurs to me that I don't know for sure, but I need to be careful tonight. If anything is going to happen between Dani and I, she should instigate it. Not me. But as my mind drifts, I can't help but picture what it would be like if Dani did instigate something between us. The way she would lean in, her chest against mine, maybe her hand slipping to the back of my neck, pulling me closer…I try to push the thought away, but it lingers.

For nearly an hour, I prowl around the club. Just as I'm about to give in and text Dani, I spot familiar blue waves. Her back is to me and she's standing on the edge of the dance floor, hips swaying gently in rhythm beneath a tight white skirt.

Fuck it. My momentary resolve flies out the window. I knock back the rest of my cocktail, set the glass on a nearby table and make my way over to her.

Resting my hands lightly on her hips, I whisper close to her ear, "Still looking for someone to kiss at midnight?"

She turns without pulling away so that we're practically nose to nose, and the breath flies right out of me—because this woman is not Dani.

She's also fucking gorgeous, and she's looking me

up and down in a way that makes my insides grip in anticipation.

"How did you know?" she asks gently in English, resting her arms lightly on my shoulders. Her brown eyes are flecked with gold and her glossy red lips are slightly parted in a teasing smile. A light smattering of freckles covers her bare arms.

"I'm sorry," I say, my hands tightening on her hips even as I try to explain my mistake. "I thought you were—"

"Hey, Brock…bra…kabra…abracadabra!" Katya bumps into me, giggling as Josh attempts to hold her upright. They both reek of vodka.

"You found her!" Josh yells, pointing at the woman in the blue wig. "Awesome. What's your name?"

The woman looks amused. "Eden."

"Eden," I echo. "This is Eden."

Josh whistles. "Wow, definitely worth it, Bracha. Way to go."

"Hang on, hang on…" Katya's speech is slurred, but she studies the woman seriously. "We gotta make sure you hit all the points on the list."

"List?" Eden clasps her fingers loosely behind my neck and gives me another sexy smile. "What list is this?"

Maybe it's the vodka. Maybe it's the music. Maybe it's the fact that I'm standing here at the very end of the worst year of my life and all I want is to leave all the pain and grief and anger behind and go home with someone new. Whatever it is, I'm suddenly filled with courage that borders on recklessness. I face Eden and tell her the truth.

"A list of qualities for my ideal wife."

She blinks. "Oh. Interesting."

The music shifts to something with a faster tempo but Eden pulls me closer as if it's a slow song.

"You want to get married?" Her voice is low and throaty.

"Is that a general question, or a proposal?" I counter with a smile. "To the former—yes. To the latter…ask me again after another drink."

Eden chuckles, and I'm mesmerised by the sound.

"Okay, Miss Eden," Katya says loudly. "Are you Jewish?"

"You can't just ask people stuff like that," Josh chides her at the same time as Eden replies, "I am."

Katya nods approvingly. "What's your…living? I mean, do you job anywhere? No… you know what I mean. Work!"

"I'm a lawyer," Eden says, glancing at me. "Building my practice."

"Wow." I immediately chide myself for the ridiculous response, then wince when Josh sticks a finger right in Eden's face.

"You got a crazy family?" he asks.

I groan whilst Eden is laughing.

"On the contrary, they're boring. In fact, I'm having dinner with my parents this weekend."

"Babies!" Katya hollers, attracting several stares. "Want?"

"Okay, I think that's enough!" I say, steering Eden

away from Josh and Katya.

"Bracha is the *best*," Katya practically yells in the highest Hebrew I have ever heard. "I'd totally marry her if I wasn't hopelessly straight."

"Same," Josh adds, although his glazed-over eyes are trained on Katya. "I'd marry her if I wasn't tragically anti-marriage."

Katya faces him again, batting her eyelashes. "Are you, though?"

In response, Josh yanks her into a kiss that earns a few whoops from the crowd. Laughing, I turn back to Eden. "Sorry about my friends."

Eden waves a hand. "It's cute. They're looking out for you. And for the record, I do want children one day." She moves closer, her lips next to my ear, and her whispered words send a warmth down my neck. "Well? Do I meet all of your criteria?"

I trace my hands further around her hips and down, and her smile widens. "So far, you seem pretty perfect," I say.

Eden glances over my shoulder and sighs. "Looks like my friends are ready to move on to the next club," she says. I look over to see three women and two men, all dressed in white with blue wigs, standing near the doorway. When I turn back to Eden, she's watching me closely. "Bracha…did you really make that list?"

I pull the list from my pocket and show her. Eden reads it closely and I find myself holding my breath. She lifts her gaze to meet mine again.

"Interesting," she whispers again.

I've only just met Eden. But all I want is to leave

with her.

"Would you like to have coffee with me tomorrow?" I say finally.

She doesn't even hesitate. "I'd love to."

"The Galya, near the Tayelet?"

"I know it." Eden touches my arm. "Eleven o'clock?"

"Great."

I watch as she moves over to her friends. One of the guys slings his arm around her shoulders and I notice a few of them glance back at me as they head out. Just before the doors swing closed, Eden looks back at me.

Her smile lingers after she's disappeared, like the bright neon spots that dance in your vision when you look up at the sun.

Blinking, I slowly look around. Club Who is packed wall to wall now and over the bar a massive digital clock has appeared, counting down the remaining forty-two minutes until midnight. The frenetic energy is contagious, and I make my way back onto the dance floor, arms high over my head. After a few minutes of winding through the bodies, I find Josh and Katya.

"Where's your wife?" Katya cries, looking around.

"Left with her friends." I pause, smiling. "But we've got a date tomorrow."

"Hell yeah!" Josh pumps his fist and hoots, while Katya throws her arms around me.

"I knew it!" she yells directly in my ear. "I *knew* you'd meet her tonight! Didn't I say so?"

"You said so," I say, giving her a tight squeeze.

For the next half hour, I obey the command of heavy techno bellowing through the speakers. A few minutes before midnight, sweaty and breathless, I peel myself away from Josh and Katya.

"Be right back!" I promise, then hurry off to find the restroom.

I'm still humming the song under my breath as I wash my hands, then splash a little cold water on my neck. When I throw the crumpled paper towel in the rubbish bin by the door, I freeze.

There's a blue wig sitting on top of the pile of towels. A blue wig with distinctly tousled layers.

"Shit," I whisper, touching the strands. "Shit. Shit. *Shit*"

I whip out my phone and open the messages app. *I'm here! Where are you?*

My stomach clenches. Dani sent the text over an hour ago, when I was…shit, shit, *shit*.

I close my eyes. I can't help but imagine it. Dani walking into the club, making her way to the dance floor, looking around for me the same way I'd looked for her. I picture her scanning the crowd, the way her expression might have changed from hopeful to something else when she spotted Eden and me with our bodies pressed close together, whispering to one another like we were the only people in the club. I picture her turning, heading for the restroom. I picture her standing in front of the sinks, staring at her reflection in the warped mirror, thinking about Riley and her bullshit excuses, me and my empty flirtations. I picture her ripping off the wig, chucking it in the rubbish bin, and leaving.

I picture all of that and for a moment, I think I might drown in guilt.

Then I snap out of it.

"What were your plans for tonight, anyway?" I ask the wig. "Hook up with me because you're upset that your girlfriend's cheating on you? Was that it?"

The door swings open, and two drunk girls in crooked white wigs stumble in, cackling loudly. I shake my head and walk out of the restroom. My mind is whirling as I search for Josh and Katya. I have nothing to feel guilty about. It's not my fault Dani's relationship is a mess. If we'd hooked up tonight, it would have made everything worse—not just between her and Riley but between us too. Our friendship— and we *are* friends, I knew that much—would've been ruined.

"This is for the best," I say out loud.

"Ten! Nine! Eight!"

Startled, I glance at the digital clock. As the raucous crowd counts down the final seconds of the year, I push my way through the masses calling Katya's name.

"Three…two…ONE! Happy New Year!"

A whirlwind of sparkling white confetti descends as everyone screams and cheers. I squeeze between two hulking men and finally spot Josh and Katya locked in a passionate kiss.

I watch them for a moment, then look away. Everyone is hugging, kissing, laughing, celebrating the new year with someone they love.

I'm standing in the middle of all of it and yet somehow, I've never felt so alone.

Chapter Eleven

I'm not one for New Year's resolutions or adhering to some abstract time frame for resolving something. But when I wake up the next morning with a pounding headache and the vague feeling that the walls are tilting around me, I say mine out loud.

"No more drinking. Period."

Hazy scenes from last night play like a movie reel in my mind as I take a boiling hot shower. Only two images are crystal clear: Eden's smile full of promise as she left the club and Dani's blue wig discarded in the rubbish bin. I focus on the first one as I finish getting ready. Anticipation is vastly preferable to guilt.

But guilt is waiting for me in the lobby.

"Morning." Dani gives me a smile that doesn't reach her eyes. She looks exhausted and I stop myself from saying so just in time.

"Hey." I pause in front of the reception desk, mildly surprised to see the magazines are neatly stacked for once. "Sorry we didn't meet up last night."

Dani lets out a dry laugh. "Are you?"

A flush creeps over my neck. "Well, yes," I say. "I got your message, but I didn't see you. The club was packed, wasn't it?"

"Mm-hmm." Dani picks up the magazines, stacks them again, and sets them down. "So, did you have a good time?"

There's an edge of sarcasm to her tone that makes

me grit my teeth. After all, I didn't do anything wrong last night. I'm not the one who may or may not have been intending to cheat on my girlfriend. I'm about to tell Dani as much when my phone buzzes.

"Ah." The word *Dad* lights up my screen, and my stomach clenches.

Dani sees it too and her eyes soften. "I hope everything's okay."

"Thanks," I mumble, hurrying into the hall for a little privacy. Bracing myself, I swipe to accept the call. "Dad? What's up?"

"Good morning! And should I say Happy Sylvester, daughter!" Dad's voice booms through the speaker and I wince, holding the phone a few inches away.

"Happy Sylvester Dad," I echo as the pounding in my temples resumes.

"How was your night? Do anything fun?"

"Went to a Novi God party."

"Oh?" His tone turns teasing. "Meet anyone interesting?"

I picture Eden in her wild blue wig and deep brown eyes.

"Just went with some friends," I reply. "How about you?"

"Oh, you know me. Quiet evening at home. One glass of champagne at midnight, in bed by twelve fifteen."

"Ha." I'm trying and failing to hide my impatience. "So, what's going on?"

"Nothing! Just had a quick question about the

house, Mum's house."

My house. I take a deep breath. "What about it?"

There's a forced lightness to Dad's tone now. "When was the last termite inspection?"

"Why?"

"Oh, well, Aggie called yesterday about some repairs, and we were just trying to—"

"*Why?*" I cut him off, heat spreading through my chest. "Why did Aggie call *you*? It's my house, Dad. I'm managing the repairs. Have been doing so for the last year. I don't recall anyone else stepping up when Mum got sick."

Dad sighs. "I know that, Bracha. But you're not here and…"

He trails off and I squeeze the phone hard. "And what?"

The silence is heavy. Eli's presence is like an invisible weight setting over the conversation. Neither of us wants to be the first to mention him, but we both know he's there.

"And we're just trying to help out," Dad finishes at last. "All of us."

"Well, I don't need your help," I tell him. "I'll manage the house when I get back. Please tell *everyone* they don't need to worry about it."

"Got it." Dad pauses. "Bracha, what's really going on?"

I frown. "What do you mean?"

"I mean, when my daughter spontaneously packs up and heads to Israel without so much as a word, I can't help but worry a little," he says quietly. "Is everything okay?"

"Everything's fine." I struggle to keep my patience. "Just because I decided to take a holiday doesn't mean anything's wrong."

"I know that I just wondered if maybe you were—"

"Dad, I promise I'm fine," I say sharply. "I'm sorry, but my, um, my taxi is here. I'll call you later, okay?"

I hang up before he can respond. After taking a minute to collect myself, I return to the lobby to find Omer seated behind the reception desk.

"Happy Sylvester, Bracha!" he calls.

"Same to you." I glance around at the otherwise empty lobby. "Where'd Dani go?"

Omer's smile fades, "Ah, she had to leave."

"Already? That was a short shift." I try to sound off-handed and fail miserably.

"She got a phone call," Omer tells me. "Family business."

"Oh." I wait for him to elaborate but he doesn't. "Okay."

The phone in the office jangles loudly and Omer leaps to his feet. "Have a great day!" He calls over his shoulder.

"You too," I say, but he's already closed the door.

***

David greets me with a steaming black coffee the moment I step into the cafe.

"I have a good feeling about this one," he says knowingly.

Nervous, I follow his gaze over to my usual table. Eden is already there, watching me with that bewitching twinkle in her eyes.

I exhale, pushing Dani out of my mind. "So do I," I tell David and he winks.

In the clear light of day without the Novi God costume, Eden is somehow even more spectacular. A slim silver barrette pins her chestnut hair back on one side so that the thick waves tumble over her shoulder. A snug grey sweater tucked into high-waisted jeans shows off her hourglass figure. She wears simple gold-hoop earrings, and her make-up is tasteful yet minimal.

I smooth down my hair, grateful I spent a little extra time on my own appearance this morning. "Hello again," Eden says as I sit down, "Nice to meet you, properly."

Half an hour later, I can't believe how well this is going. Eden seems to want to know everything about me and her questions about my life in Australia, my career, and my family are endless—yet somehow, never feel too invasive or prying. For a little while, I'm tense, almost as if I'm waiting for something to give. But before long, I find myself telling Eden about my mother, about Eli and the house, even about my phone call with Dad earlier.

"I'm sure your attorney covered his bases when it comes to Eli being of sound mind," Eden says, running a finger along the rim of her coffee mug.

"But you might consider contesting your mother's will."

I frown slightly. "In what way?"

"You mentioned she suffered from depression in her final years," Eden says matter-of-factly. "There might be some way to demonstrate she wasn't of sound mind when she decided to leave half her estate to her incarcerated son."

I'm taken aback by the suggestion that Mum "wasn't of sound mind." Eden must see it in my expression because she reaches out and touches my hand.

"I'm sorry if I offended you," she says. "I slipped into lawyer mode."

I relax a little. "No, it's fine. I appreciate the advice. And I honestly don't care about Eli getting half of Mum's money. It's the house I'm worried about."

"What's the property value?" Eden asks.

I shift in my chair. "Why?"

"Just curious as to why you don't want to sell."

"Because it's my home."

Eden nods slowly. "You want to start your own family there? With your perfect wife?"

I relax because that teasing smile from last night is back. "It's crossed my mind, yes," I reply, matching her tone.

"That's cute," Eden says, nudging her foot against mine under the table. "But would you be open to another proposal?"

There's a suggestive hint to the way she says

proposal. "I'm all ears," I say, scooting my chair closer. A moment later, I feel her hand rest lightly on my knee.

"If you were my client, my advice would be to sell the house," Eden says. "No more house, no more stress with your brother and his plans. Money equals freedom, Bracha." She pauses, then adds, "It's the logical move."

I can't argue with that. Even though I love Mum's house, it's sentimental, it isn't logical to keep a house that needs so much work when starting a new family and a new life. A voice in my head is insisting that sentiment doesn't need logic to be important—a voice that sounds a lot like Dani, which is why I decide to ignore it.

"Fair point, counsellor," I say, and Eden rewards me with a wide smile. "You know, I could use a little more legal advice. Maybe over dinner?"

The rest of the day is just like Eden—almost too good to be true. We take a long walk on the beach and it's my turn to interrogate her. I listen as she talks about how her grandmother inspired her to go to law school, how her mother established a career as a real estate agent before marrying her father and having children, and how she wants to do the same. Over dinner at a Moroccan restaurant Eden chooses, we share a chickpea dish as she tells me all the steps she's taken to launch her own practice next year. When a baby at the next table begins to wail, and Eden leans over, I brace myself, remembering my disastrous date with Abby.

But Eden simply picks up the small, tattered blanket on the floor and places it on the table. She smiles and the baby coos as his mother thanks Eden profusely.

She turns back to me and plucks an olive off the plate. "Isn't he the cutest?" she says. "Just perfect."

"Perfect," I repeat and I'm not talking about the baby.

When we leave the restaurant, Eden invites me to her place for a nightcap. I say yes without hesitation.

Hours later, I'm sprawled on top of her sheets staring at the ceiling as Eden takes a shower. The sex was…

I cast around for the right word.

Good. Fine. Successful.

Clinical comes to mind. Everything was done precisely, correctly. I'm satisfied.

Technically.

I wonder briefly if it was a mistake to rush into the bedroom on the first date but as Eden had pointed out, the moment she'd closed her front door and slid her hands under my shirt, surely there needed to be a point on my list for sex?

She was right, of course. Better to know sooner rather than later. And it was…good.

Fine.

Successful.

The sound of running water cuts off abruptly and Eden steps out of the bathroom. "Hey, are you busy tomorrow?"

I can't help but smile at the sight of her towelling

her hair dry, completely naked.

"No. Why?"

"I mentioned this Friday is my grandparent's fiftieth anniversary," Eden says, wrapping the damp towel around her waist. "They're having a celebration at their house. Would you like to come?"

"Oh." I sit up, studying her. "They'd be okay with that? You bringing along a date you just met?"

"Are you kidding?" Eden heads back into the bathroom. "I'm dating a successful Australian doctor! They would be angry with me for not introducing you sooner!"

I laugh, resting back against the pillows. "In that case, I'd love to."

Chapter Twelve

I spend the night at Eden's place. In the morning, we sit at the little table on her balcony and she serves a bowl of figs and almonds before she heads off to work.

The whole thing is…well…odd. Not in a bad way, exactly. I've had plenty of one-night stands and I never stay for breakfast. But she and I both know this is different. Maybe that's what makes it strange. Eden knows why I'm in Israel. She knows my plan. And so far, she seems to be on board. But the fact is, we barely know each other, and sitting across from her, wearing one of her cotton bathrobes and stirring my black coffee grains, I feel almost like we're playing house.

"Don't forget your phone," Eden says as we're getting ready to leave. "It's plugged in next to the sofa."

"Thanks." I retrieve my phone, which was a useless brick when I woke up. My chest tightens when I see the notifications on the screen—one from Dad and several from an unfamiliar number.

I kiss Eden goodbye, like we've already been in a steady relationship for a year, and order a taxi. Once I'm settled in the backseat, I open the messages app. I scan Dad's quickly—it's a screenshot with flight info along with a lengthy message about a trip he's taking. I shoot back a thumbs up before moving on to the other texts.

There are at least a dozen of them, some with

photos. I read the first message and utter a swear that causes the driver to eye me in the rearview mirror.

Hey, sis. Checking out the house and have a few questions for you.

How the actual fuck did Eli get my number? Immediately, I know the answer: Dad.

Furious, I scroll through the messages.

This rust is insane, gotta get on that.

Did you know about this mould?

Did Mum have tradesmen come check this out regularly?

Most are accompanied by photos, an up-close slideshow of each and every flaw in the house. By the time I get to the end of the texts, I'm literally shaking with rage.

I will not rise to this bait. Instead, I text Leo.

Is Eli still there? Why didn't you change the locks??!

I wait an agonising two minutes for his response.

At work. I did change them. Aggie's at the house, she must've let him in. Call you later.

"Fuck!" I yell, and the driver glares at me.

I mumble an apology and make sure to leave the maximum tip but I'm still seeing red as I storm through the doors.

Dani leaps back, paintbrush in hand. "Whoa!"

"Sorry." I glance at the wall, where she's adding a rather psychedelic fish to the mural. Then I look back at her and realise her eyes are pink. As if she's been crying. Again.

"So." Dani glances pointedly at my shirt and jeans. "I take it you had a nice evening?"

"What?"

"That's what you were wearing yesterday."

"Oh." I shrug and do my best to sound not-smug. "Yeah, I had a date."

Dani resumes painting. "With the woman you met at Club Who?"

"Yes. Her name's Eden."

"And she's a nine-point woman?"

I know she's teasing but I take the question seriously. Eden does indeed meet all the points on my list. What's more, she knows about my list, my search and it hasn't put her off. Quite the opposite, in fact.

"She is," I say finally. "So far, at least, she's pretty much…perfect."

Dani's brush stops moving for a fraction of a second. Then, she begins adding texture to the gills with quick, hurried strokes. "Well, congratulations. Mission accomplished."

There's no mistaking the bitterness in her voice. I'm silent for a moment, trying to think of the right thing to say to cheer her up.

"You know, two New Year's Eves ago, my friend Maddy invited me to a massive party at a beach house," I say finally. "The kind of party that starts New Year's Eve. So, you know? But that morning, there was a massive accident on the highway. Seven cars and a bus. Massive injuries, a few really critical. I ended up working nearly forty hours straight. I have no recollection of midnight coming or going. And I found out later, Maddy was actually kind of upset with me for bailing on her. Even though she knew I didn't have a choice."

Slowly, Dani lowers her arm and turns to face me. Her brows are pinched together. "What exactly are you trying to say?"

I shrug. "Just that it's okay to be upset that Riley didn't come, but that doesn't mean her reason isn't, you know…valid." I lie.

Dani stares at me, her expression unreadable. "I appreciate that, Bracha, but honestly? I've got bigger things to worry about than my girlfriend's stupid work schedule."

I try a smile. "Like what? Adding a whale to the mural?"

Dani presses her lips together tightly. I watch as her brush flicks, flicks, flicks at the fish and though her movements are frantic and rushed, the resulting gills are astounding in their careful detail. When she finally speaks, her voice is barely above a whisper.

"My grandfather has entered palliative care."

My breath catches in my throat. Visions of Mum float in my mind, the day I tucked her into her bed at home after her last stay at the hospital. She smiled weakly and said how glad she was to be here, that this was just what she needed. But she looked all withered and grey-skinned, like a corpse in waiting, and I'd hurried off to make some tea before she could see the tears in my eyes.

"Oh, Dani. I'm so sorry." I pause. "Is he at home?"

She nods, dipping her brush into a little vial of green paint. "His house. I've been pretty much living there for the last few months. My landlord probably thinks I've abandoned my apartment but I just had this feeling that I don't know…that the more time I spent with him, the more I could prolong his life." Dani casts a sidelong look at me. "Impractical, I know."

"No, I get it." I take a deep breath. "I felt the same way about my Mum in those last weeks. It was almost like…I don't know. As long as I was there, I could keep her alive."

Dani's mouth relaxes slightly. "That's exactly how it feels."

I smile, and for the first time in what feels like forever, a genuine smile lights up Dani's face.

"I'm really sorry about your grandfather. I know how hard this part is."

She studies me in a way that causes something to flare up deep in my stomach. "Got any plans this afternoon?"

"Not a thing."

Dani hesitates, twirling the paintbrush between her fingers. "Would you maybe like to meet him?"

***

After a late morning nap and coffee that afternoon, I meet Dani outside the hostel. The weather is unusually warm, so we decide to skip the bus and walk. As we do, I listen quietly as Dani tells me all about her grandfather. How he survived the Holocaust but lost his entire family. How he escaped on a boat when he was only fourteen, that no one in his family believed him when he said what was coming. He eventually started his own family here.

"Speaking of families," Dani says, glancing at me. "How's everything with yours? Any news about your brother?"

I grimace, thinking of the texts. "He's out of prison and in my house. And he has a few ideas on how to fix things up."

Dani winces. "Tough."

"Yeah." I think about Eden's advice to sell the house. "I don't know what to do. Legally, he's not doing anything wrong…yet, anyway. But it's just…"

"It's your home," Dani says softly, and my throat tightens.

"Exactly."

When we reach her grandfather's house—a modest, white one-story with a small but well-groomed yard—Dani touches my arm.

"His name's Solomon, but call him Sol," she says. "And you might have to introduce yourself more than once. He's…you know."

"Yeah. I know."

Sol Rosenberg has to be the feistiest hospice patient I've ever met.

We find him sitting up in bed, chatting away with the dark-haired nurse clearing away his lunch plate. When he sees Dani, his face lights up with a smile so similar to hers, it almost brings tears to my eyes.

"Hello, Daniella!" he says in Hebrew. His gaze flits over to me. "And who is this?"

Dani opens her mouth, but I beat her to it. "I'm

Bracha, a friend of Daniella's," I wink at Dani, "So nice to meet you, Sol."

My accent isn't flawless, but my Hebrew is otherwise perfect. Dani gives me a smile as Sol waves me over to the chair next to his bed.

For the next two hours, Sol entertains us with stories, many of which are different versions of an incident involving a fortune teller he met on the beach during a matkot competition when a rogue ball ended up flying into her booth.

"She swore it knocked her right here," Sol tells me eagerly, tapping his forehead. "Right in the third eye! And that was when she had a vision of me with my dear Esther. Met her the very next day!"

"Incredible," I say as I rewrap the bandage around his wrist.

"Proposed within a week," he rattles on. "Because I knew she was the one. When you know, you know…you know?"

I can't help but laugh, and Dani does as well.

"Do you believe in fortune telling, Bracha?" Sol asks.

Dani giggles and I give her an innocent smile. "I'm afraid that's not really my sort of thing."

"Ah, that doesn't matter." Sol pats my arm with his frail hand. "It's the beautiful thing about fate, it is destined to happen because we make it happen."

I smile at him, aware of Dani listening closely.

"That's the thing Sol," I say, enunciating my Hebrew carefully. "We make it happen."

***

Sol's words stay with me.

It wasn't Sol's story about how he'd met his wife that got me. It was his *belief.* Usually, I'd be rolling my eyes at anyone who insisted a psychic predicted the meet-cute with their future partner, but Sol was just so earnest, so pure, so determined.

"I set eyes on Esther, and I thought, *there she is,*" Sol had told me, his eyes glazed over. "Right on time. Proposed a week later. Why waste time when you know you've found the one?"

I'm still thinking about him when Eden and I arrive at her grandparents' house.

"Everything okay?" Eden asks as we stroll up the walk. Unlike Sol's modest home, the Vaknin estate is a three-story modern affair with floor-to-ceiling windows and a minimalist design. "You seem distracted."

"It's nothing," I reply, reaching for her hand. "You look stunning, did I mention?"

Eden preens in a self-mocking way. "You did, but continue."

"You look *stunning.*"

And she does, wearing an off-the-shoulder burgundy silk dress with a fluted skirt that shows off every curve. It coordinates perfectly with the black-and-tan trousers and fitted vest over a crisp white blouse that I've chosen. Well, that Eden's chosen for me. She has excellent taste in fashion and I didn't exactly pack anything suitable for a wealthy couple's fiftieth anniversary party.

Nerves flutter in my stomach as Eden escorts me into an impeccably polished foyer. Everything gleams, from the white marble floor to the crystal chandelier overhead.

"Eden, my dear!" A beautiful woman with grey-streaked brown hair tied into an elegant top knot swoops in and pulls Eden into a hug. "Everyone's inside. And this must be Bracha!"

She holds out her hand and I shake it firmly. "It's so nice to meet you, Mrs. Blum."

Her eyes widen and she lets out a delighted laugh. "Oh, you're a smooth one, aren't you?"

Confused, I look at Eden, who seems amused. "This isn't my mother, Bracha," she explains with a little wink. "She's my grandmother."

"Oh!" I can tell from their expressions that they think I'm having a little fun with them. But the truth is, I can't believe this striking woman is Eden's grandmother. She doesn't look a day over forty. "In that case, nice to meet you, Mrs. Vaknin."

"Nice one," Eden whispers, and I shrug and smile as we move into the salon.

A few dozen guests are already milling around, sipping wine and picking delicacies from the catering table. I'm swarmed in seconds and for the next half hour, I do my best to keep everyone straight: Mr. Vaknin, who looks every bit as youthful and vibrant as his wife, along with Eden's parents, her brother Asher and his wife Sarah and Mrs. Vaknin's two *older* sisters (which she is quick to point out with a teasing grin) only serves to drive home the point that Eden won the genetic lottery.

It isn't long before I realise nearly everyone here is some type of success story. Asher is a lawyer, Sarah is in Real Estate, Mr Vaknin is a retired lawyer and now adjunct professor.

"An ER doctor, now *that's* impressive," Mrs. Vaknin says as she refills my glass with merlot. "It must be terribly stressful working in such an environment."

"It can be," I reply. "But I thrive in high-pressure situations. I'd imagine it's similar to the thrill you must get defending clients in court."

"Oh, absolutely!" Mr. Vaknin booms, loosening his black tie. "The only reason I took up jet-skiing was so I could chase that courtroom high since I retired!"

"What was the most interesting case of your career?" I ask, plucking a stuffed olive from a silver platter.

Mr. Vaknin chuckles. "Oh, easy. I had a client whose wife had filed for divorce and sole custody of the children based on the grounds that he was possessed by a 'malicious spirit with ill intent.'"

I choke on a piece of walnut. "I'm sorry?"

Everyone laughs as he launches into the story for what I'm sure is not the first time. But as he talks, my mind wanders back to Sol and his silly, sweet tale of the fortune teller who predicted he'd meet his future wife in a week. When Mr. Vaknin finishes, I join in the laughter a beat too late.

"Well, not every couple makes it fifty years,"

Asher says, slipping his arm around Sarah.

"Too true," Eden agrees. And slips her arm around my waist.

It doesn't take me long to sense a quiet current of status in the room, its sheen brushing dangerously close to the superficial.

I fight the urge to text Leo. *I've met the woman I'm going to marry. She's beautiful, she's smart, her family is successful, she ticks every point on the list, but…*

"What is it?" Eden asks, and now all eyes are on me.

I clear my throat. "Oh, just wondering if the happy couple has any advice for the rest of us who are hoping for a successful marriage."

That gets a chuckle from everyone and Eden gives me an approving smile.

"Seconded!" Sarah pipes up, raising her glass. "I'd love some words of wisdom."

Mr. and Mrs. Vaknin share a knowing look. They turn and smile at their children and grandchildren and say, in perfect unison:

"Get a pre-nup."

Everyone bursts out laughing. I join in, although secretly, I'd been hoping for something more…inspirational. Maybe something about destiny, love, or even writing a list would suffice at this point.

I shake off the thought. Frankly, pre-nups are the logical choice. And Eden's family are logical. Rational. Ambitious. Drama-free.

Perfect. *Right?*

"They love you," she whispers in my ear as her

grandfather uncorks another bottle of merlot. "Well done."

She squeezes my hand and we hold out our glasses for refills. *This is perfect,* I tell myself over and over again. *Eden is perfect. She's the one. This is so right. When you know, you know.*

You know?

Chapter Thirteen

I know.

It all works out on paper. Eden ticks every box, meets every criteria. I know she's the one, because it's only logical. So, I commit, full-stop. And every time I have the fleeting thought that *this is moving too fast* or *does this really feel right?* I remind myself that this isn't about feelings. The feelings that aren't there yet will fall into place. I know they will.

You know?

For our third date, Eden meets me at the hostel. More specifically, in the lobby. Where Dani is working. I walk in and momentarily freeze at the sight of Eden near the entrance casually chatting with Dani. It's almost an Odd Couple effect: Eden, effortlessly chic in a basic black dress with heels, gold necklace, and matching bracelet, hair swept into a sleek bun; and Dani, back in her paint-spattered overalls, auburn hair in a messy ponytail, squatting and wielding a brush she's using to add an electric eel above the baseboard.

"That sounds a little depressing," Dani is saying. Neither of them has noticed me yet. "Doesn't it mess with your head, when you have to work with couples whose relationships are doomed?"

"Quite the opposite," Eden replies, stepping back to avoid paint spatter as Dani swipes the brush vigorously. "I believe it's made me more clear-eyed when it comes to my own relationships. I know what

I want. It usually comes down to that in my experience. When a couple decides on divorce, it's because they entered the marriage without having clearly defined goals of what they both wanted."

Dani unscrews a bottle of purple paint. "Maybe they don't know," she points out. "Not everyone knows what they want in life. But you meet someone and you just…want to figure it out together. So, you follow your heart."

Eden gives her a condescending smile that I'm glad Dani can't see. "Yes, that's true. But statistically speaking, what they'll figure out is that they made a mistake."

Dani's shoulders tense, but she doesn't respond.

"Take my current client," Eden goes on. "Her husband wanted to pursue a career in advertising and she supported that. Even when it meant he started spending more and more time at the office, sometimes even overnight. Turns out he was sleeping with his boss."

Dani drops her paintbrush, cursing under her breath.

"Eden!" I call, hurrying forward. "You're early."

"I thought we could walk to the wine bar," Eden says, reaching for my hand. "It's nice out and I've been held up at the office all day."

"That sounds great." I pause, glancing at Dani. "Um…I see you've met Eden?"

"I have." Dani gives me a smile that doesn't reach her eyes. "We had a nice chat. You two certainly seem perfect for one another. Goals and all."

Eden squeezes my hand but I just look at Dani. Her words were complimentary. But her tone decidedly wasn't.

"Thanks," I say finally. "Well…have a good night."

"You too."

She returns to her eel and I walk out the doors with Eden without looking back.

We start the evening at a romantic wine bar Eden chose, where we share a bottle of rosé at a cosy, candlelit table for two. Eden does most of the talking, mostly because my mind keeps wandering back to Dani. Specifically, her reaction to Eden's story about the client with the cheating husband.

She knows Riley is messing around. Or at least, she suspects it. So why doesn't she just break things off? She deserves so much better.

After the wine bar, Eden brings me to a nearby art gallery.

"They're hosting an exhibition of an up-and-coming local's work tonight," Eden tells me as we stroll arm-in-arm across the intersection. "Everyone in my circle has been buzzing about him. Very minimalist. My friend Dina recently purchased one of his paintings and it's breathtaking."

Very minimalist, it turns out, is an understatement.

The massive canvases along the walls are white, save for a small geometric shape in black: a circle in the top left corner, a trapezoid clinging to the top of the canvas, a blue triangle dead centre.

"Striking," I say at last, picturing Dani's vivid,

colourful murals.

"Isn't it?" But Eden isn't looking at the giant painting of a tiny square in front of us. When I turn, I realise she's gazing around at the few dozen people milling around the gallery, sipping champagne, and chatting in hushed tones. A man with a salt-and-pepper beard catches her eye and waves, and Eden lights up.

"Who's that?" I ask as she pulls me across the gallery.

"Judge Abrams," she says eagerly. "I've tried a few cases in front of him. Very well-respected. I'd love to introduce you."

For the next hour or so, we chat with a group of what I gather are very wealthy, very well-connected people. Eden is poised and charming and I can't help but admire the way she effortlessly captures everyone's attention with her words.

"Six new client requests this week," she says with a cheeky smile. "And next week will be double that. We've definitely hit a busy month."

Her colleagues chuckle and I look at her questioningly. "Why do you think that is?"

"The winter, shifting priorities, new...whatever," Eden says waiving her hand like she's dismissing a waiter. "Parents fighting over custody agreements, prenuptial renegotiations, estate planning disasters. Some just want a fresh start."

Eden speaks in a clinical, cold manner and she must feel my shock as she places her hand on mine and gives it a squeeze.

"It's one of the busiest months for any family law practice," an olive-skinned woman in a sky-blue cocktail dress tells me. "Doesn't matter if it's a guardianship battle or just parents trying to recalibrate their co-parenting agreements, the winter tensions usually rise up and by January everyone has had enough."

"It's almost always the same reason, when you really boil it down," Eden points out. "Lack of communication and not being on the same page." She raises her glass to me, eyes sparkling. "Which is why I think you've got something special Bracha, that list of yours is incredibly logical—know exactly what you want in a partner based off common goals and traits and you will be sure to succeed. Luckily, I match every point."

I can't help but smile as Eden winks at me and places a warm kiss on my chin.

"If more people approached relationships like this, rather than just…" Eden curls her fingers into air quotes. "*Following their hearts,* there would be a lot less heartache."

That gets a chuckle from the crowd and I force an awkward one as well. But I can't help but flinch on Dani's behalf. Because those were Dani's exact words earlier.

Eden is right, of course. Dani is choosing to stay in a long-distance relationship with a woman who is most likely cheating. It isn't logical.

When you know, you know. You know?

Hours later, Eden and I return to the hostel, tipsy

on champagne. I'm both relieved and disappointed to see that the lobby is empty. I lead Eden to my room and close the door. As she slips off her dress, I see denim overalls and paint-spattered skin.

"Come here," she whispers, and I do.

But as we tumble into bed and I close my eyes, it isn't Eden I'm reaching for.

***

My phone buzzes at 5 a.m. I roll over and see its Dad.

"Everything okay?" Eden mumbles.

"Just my dad forgetting time zones exist," I reply, slipping my arm around her waist. Within a minute, I'm asleep again.

An hour later: *Buzz-buzz.*

Thirty minutes after that: *Buzz-buzz.*

"Ugh." I sit up, rubbing my eyes. Next to me, Eden stretches and yawns.

"It's no big deal," she says, tossing off the blanket. "I've got a meeting in a few hours. I should get—"

Knock-knock. We both look at my door. But before either of us can move, it swings open.

"Rise and shine!" Dani says cheerfully. "You've got a surprise…um. Visitor."

Before I can process the extreme awkwardness that is Dani standing in my doorway, staring at a fully naked Eden and me in bed, she moves aside to reveal my father.

"Dad?" I choke, pulling my shirt on backward.

"Why…what are you…"

My brain is short-circuiting. For his part, Dad doesn't look shocked. His expression of mild surprise has already shifted into one of amusement as his thick, black moustache curves up at his lips.

"Well, I did try calling you a few times, Bracha," he says mildly. "Now I see why you weren't answering."

"I'm so sorry," Dani pipes up, her cheeks bright red. "I didn't realise you were…um…I thought you were…alone"

I cannot believe this is happening. And Dani has no idea just how bad it is. How could I possibly explain to her—or to Eden—that I, a fully grown woman, have yet to come out to my father?

With a little laugh, Eden stands and wraps the blanket around her like a sleeveless dress. "It's no problem at all," she says smoothly, holding the blanket in place with one hand and reaching out to my dad with the other. "I'm so happy to meet you, Mr. Cohen!"

"And I'm glad to meet you, er…" Dad glances at me as he shakes Eden's hand.

"Eden," I manage to say.

"Eden." Dad smiles. "Lovely name."

"Thank you!" Eden looks completely at ease, as if this isn't the most mortifying thing that has ever happened. "I'll just go clean up."

She grabs her dress and swans out of the room. My eyes flick from Dani to Dad.

"I'll be going too," Dani blurts out. "Sorry again

for, um, interrupting."

She closes the door behind her, leaving Dad and I alone.

"So," I say.

"So," Dad says.

"I guess now you know."

Dad frowns slightly. "Know?"

"You know…" I swallow. *When you know, you know.* "That I like women. Sorry, I never told you."

"Oh." To my surprise, Dad laughs. "Bracha, my daughter. Just because you didn't tell me doesn't mean I didn't know."

I have no idea what to say to that. "Okay. Well. So. What are you doing here?"

Dad tilts his head. "You inspired me to make a trip home. Didn't you see my texts? I shared my flight info."

Oh, crap. "Right. Okay."

"And I'm not here to intrude or ruin your…" Dad glances back at the door. "Fun."

"Dad—"

"I've got my own plans while I'm here. People I want to visit, all that." Dad pauses. "But I did want to talk to you, Bracha. About Eli."

My throat tightens. I don't respond.

"Coffee later?" Dad asks. "There's a cafe next door that the young receptionist mentioned, called The Galya; don't know if you've tried it."

I sigh. "A few times, yeah. I'll meet you there after I get dressed."

The moment he leaves, I pull out my phone.

I call Leo first, listening as it rings. I feel like my brain is short-circuiting, cycling from Dad finding me in bed with Eden, to Dani's strange reaction, to Eden's smooth, calm demeanour.

Leo's call goes to voice mail. Instinctively, I start to call Maddy next, then remember she still hasn't responded to my texts. Then I realise who I really need advice from right now.

This time, I get an answer after one ring.

"Hello?"

"Victoria?"

"Bracha? Hey! How's the trip going?"

The sound of my mentor's voice causes my muscles to relax slightly. Before I know it, I'm spilling the whole story, only it's all out of order—New Year's, meeting Eden, Dad's surprise arrival, Dani, Dani, Dani…

"Bracha, love." Victoria cuts me off, and her tone is no-nonsense boss. "Take a breath."

I do.

"Get your doctor switched on," she says firmly. "I gather you've got a problem. Give me an SBAR."

Nodding, I sit up straight. "Right. Situation: I'm in my hostel room. I spent the night here with Eden. This morning, Dani brought my dad up here, and they caught us in bed together. Dad didn't freak out. Dani kind of did. I'm not even wearing pants."

"Background?" Victoria prompts.

"Dad's here to visit friends, but also because he wants to talk about Eli and all the inheritance bullshit. Eden is a woman I've been dating. She's perfect.

Assessment—"

"Hang on. Background on Dani?"

"Oh." I exhale. "Dani works at the hostel. We're…friends."

When I don't elaborate, Victoria clears her throat. "Okay. Assessment?"

"I never told Dad I'm gay, but he said he knew. Dani knew I was on a date with Eden last night, but she acted all weird when she found us together."

"Hmm." Victoria is quiet for a moment. "Recommendations?"

"I should probably put on pants."

I can hear the smile in Victoria's voice when she responds. "Yes, that's wise. What else?"

"I'm going to have coffee with Dad." I make a face. "And while I don't want to talk about my brother, I know that if Dad flew all the way to Tel Aviv, it's important. So, I'm going to hear him out."

"Good. And with Eden?"

I shrug. "Eden's fine. She's perfect, actually. Seemed happy to meet my dad. No action required."

"And the hostel worker? Dani?"

I open my mouth, but nothing comes out.

"Bracha?"

"No action required," I say at last.

Victoria chuckles. "Sweetie, even I know that isn't the case. There's something you're not telling me here. If Dani had a strange reaction to finding you in bed with another woman, is it possible she has—"

"No," I cut in, because I don't want to hear her say it. "Trust me, no. She has a long-distance girlfriend.

150

And I mean, yes, she's attractive and she can be flirty but…but she's all wrong for me. And I'm all wrong for her. And Eden is perfect."

"So you keep saying."

"Because it's a fact." I squeeze the bridge of my nose. "It's a fact. So…this was helpful, Victoria. Thanks for listening. I should go talk to my dad."

"Anytime, Bracha," Victoria says. "I mean it, too. Call me if anything else comes up, okay?"

"Will do. Thanks."

I hang up and close my eyes. After a few deep breaths, I stand up and head to my closet.

"No action required," I tell myself. "Not with Eden, not with Dani."

I dress quickly, kiss Eden in the shower, and head to The Galya. I spot Dad right away—he's chosen my date table by the window, which makes me groan inwardly. He waves and I wave back before ordering a black coffee.

"So," David says, sliding the mug toward me. "I see you're trying something…ah, different?"

He glances pointedly at Dad and I laugh. "Um, no. That's my father."

"Got it."

I bring my coffee over to the table and take a seat, trying not to think about how many women had been in Dad's chair and how badly all those dates had gone.

Dad clears his throat. "Bracha, I want to say something and I just need you to listen, okay? However, you want to feel about it is fine, but please just hear me out."

"Okay," I say.

He takes a deep breath. "I didn't come here to change your mind about Eli or to force you to have a relationship with him. I came here because I want the same courtesy from you."

I stiffen. "What do you mean?"

"I mean, my relationship with my son is up to me, not you." Dad's tone is gentle but the words still cut. "I'm well aware of the choices he's made. It's something he and I have discussed at length. And I've chosen forgiveness, acceptance, and trust. You may not choose the same and that's okay. I'm not trying to make you accept him. But—"

"Aren't you?" I can't help but interrupt. "Giving him my number? Letting him in my house?"

Dad holds up a hand. "I admit, I overstepped by giving him your number," he says calmly. "I apologise. But I didn't let him into *your* house, Bracha. Your mother left that house to both of you. He has every right to enter."

I grit my teeth but say nothing.

Dad sits with ease. He has always been the kind of man who commands his presence with an unshakeable sense of self.

"That said, you and Leo have made it your home," Dad continues. "So I understand how it might feel like a violation. And that's why I'm asking that you have a conversation with your brother, Bracha. Just hear him out."

"I don't—"

"You told me a story once," Dad says loudly, and

I fall into a sullen silence. "About a patient you had during your residency. Her husband brought her in after she'd fallen down the stairs. Concussion, bruises, a broken rib. You said the physical diagnosis was quick and set about treating her. But it was only when her husband stepped out of the room that the woman admitted he had pushed her."

My stomach twists. I remember that patient in vivid detail. The fear in her eyes; the way her trembling fingers clutched my wrist as she whispered the truth in my ear.

"Her injuries hadn't changed, but the treatment did," Dad goes on. "Because it wasn't enough anymore to dress her injuries. You had to get her to safety and if her husband hadn't decided to grab something from the vending machine, she never would have given you that piece of vital information."

I close my eyes briefly. "I missed so much," I say quietly. "Looking back, there were other signs of abuse. A more experienced doctor would have noticed but I didn't."

"I remember exactly what you said that night." Dad pauses, stirring his coffee. "You said, the husband's version of the story made your assessment of her injuries subjective, rather than objective."

I sigh. "Right. And your point is?"

"I think you know exactly what my point is, Bracha." Dad reaches across the table and takes my hand. "Your assessment of your brother right now is highly subjective. Perhaps a little more objectivity is in order. That's all."

He squeezes my hand. I squeeze back, albeit a little reluctantly.

"Fine," I say. "Point taken. I'll talk to Eli. Happy?"

"Quite." Dad settles back in his chair and takes a sip of coffee. His eyes sparkle as he sets down the mug. "Now…tell me more about Eden."

I meet his gaze, doing my best not to think about the scene he walked in on this morning.

"Eden is…" I pause, picturing Mum's pale face, her shadowed eyes, that exhausted but genuine smile. *I want you to find someone, Bracha. Marriage, a family, a life…I want that for you more than anything.*

"Eden is the woman I'm going to marry," I tell Dad, and I mean it.

Chapter Fourteen

A week later, I'm more certain than ever. Eden is the one.

It's a sunny Saturday, and with the midwinter sun high in the sky, it could almost pass for warm. Eden and I are camped out in two lounge chairs on the beach. Neither of us are in swimsuits—it's not *that* warm—but Eden's cardigan is draped over the back of her chair. She's in a tank top and skirt, eyes closed beneath her stylish sunglasses as she allows the sun to kiss her bare shoulders. Which is something on my own agenda later this afternoon.

For now, I've got my bare toes in the cool sand and a novel Katya loaned me spread open on my lap. It's an interpretation of Romeo and Juliet but with a surfer and a waitress who seem like a good fit except the surfer (I'm guessing) is going to drown. I'm having trouble focusing because my mind keeps wandering back to Dani, her grandfather, the ocean, then back to Dani.

Dani, who's barely spoken to me since finding me in bed with Eden.

Dani, who hasn't posted on her socials all week.

Dani, who has a shift starting in half an hour.

Not that I'm counting the minutes or anything.

I jump when my phone buzzes.

"Everything okay?" Eden murmurs without turning her head.

I nod. "Just my dad letting me know his plane landed. He's back in Sydney."

"Ah, good." Eden yawns and stretches. "It's so nice that he flew out here. I had such a good time at breakfast the other day."

"Me too." I did have a good time, although having shakshuka with Dad and my girlfriend had been a completely surreal experience. I still hadn't admitted to Eden that I'd never come out to my father before. The truth was, now that it was all out in the open, I wasn't even sure *why*. Dad was perfectly accepting. And he'd clearly been charmed by Eden.

"He's going to do some work on the house while I'm gone," I tell her now, sliding my phone back in my pocket. "With Eli. Just basic repairs, that kind of thing."

I intend to keep my promise to Dad. But I haven't talked to Eli yet. I suspect Dad's offer to join Eli when he visits the house was just to give me peace of mind. And it does just that.

"Oh?" Eden adjusts the straps of her tank top. "That's nice. Get it all fixed up to sell."

I glance at her, surprised. Neither of us has mentioned the idea of putting the house on the market since she first suggested it. Is she assuming that's what I'm going to do? If I tell her I'm not, will she think I'm being too sentimental?

I'm not sure what to say. But apparently, Eden isn't expecting a response.

"It's nearly noon," she says, raising her sunglasses and looking at her watch. "Are you up for a little coffee before lunch? There's a little boutique cafe that just opened on Shenkin and rumour has it they have great pastries." When I give her a puzzled look, Eden grins. "Ah yes, no sweets, I remember." Then she kisses me on the cheek.

I force a smile as I get to my feet; of course, Eden knows my meal timings and dietary particulars; that's good, that's great, I force the thought.

"Would you mind if I skip the coffee and just meet you for lunch? I'm going to head back to the hostel and freshen up."

"Of course." Eden tilts her head and I plant a kiss on her cheek. She slips her hand around my neck and pulls me in for a deeper kiss. She gives me that sly smile as I straighten up. "See you in a bit."

I return the smile but it fades as soon as I turn away. I shoulder my bag, double-checking to make sure I have Katya's book as I head to the boardwalk.

This is what perfect feels like, I tell myself.

This is how it's supposed to feel.

***

There's a group of backpackers crowded around the reception desk, so I hang back for a minute.

"Down the hall, to the left!" a familiar voice calls as they finally disperse. I blink when I realise it's Katya, not Dani, who's on the other side of the desk. "Hey, lady!" she says cheerfully, waving me over. "Ooh, what do you think so far?"

She gestures at the book I'd forgotten I was

holding. "Oh! Um. Good, yeah," I say, glancing at the closed office door. "What are you doing?"

"Omer asked me to check people in while he's on a call."

"But isn't Dani supposed to be working right now?"

Katya's face falls and a wave of foreboding sweeps over me. "Yeah, she's taking some time off. A few days, I think."

"Is she sick?" I press.

Katya toys with her long-beaded necklace. "No, her grandfather passed early this morning. He'd been feeling poorly for a few days."

The news hits me like a physical blow. I actually take a step back. "He…he died?" I search my mind, trying to remember the last time I saw Dani working, but I'm coming up blank. I'd thought she was avoiding me. It hadn't even occurred to me that something might be wrong.

"You okay?" Katya asks, eyeing me closely.

My throat is too tight to answer. Fortunately, Omer chooses that moment to step out of the office.

"Bracha, my dear!" he calls, arms spread as if he hasn't seen me in years. Then he lowers his arms and tilts his head. "So you've heard?"

"I just told her," Katya tells him.

I swallow hard. "Yes, it's…terrible. I had no idea."

Because she hasn't texted or called. Because she's avoiding me. Or maybe because we're not as close as I thought we were.

Those thoughts flood my mind, followed by a hefty wave of guilt. As if Dani had a responsibility to let a woman she's known for a little over a month about her loss. Deep down, I know I have no right to feel hurt.

Omer nods gravely. "The funeral is tomorrow morning," he says. "We will all be there to support her, yes?"

Katya looks surprised. "Isn't it family only? I don't want to intrude."

Omer and I exchange knowing looks. "Jewish funeral," Omer tells her. "All are welcome and encouraged to attend. I know Dani would love to see her hostel family there. Please tell Josh, as well," he adds to Katya.

She glances at me. "And it wouldn't be inappropriate?"

I shake my head. "No," I say honestly. "Dani would appreciate it. I'm going."

I say the words before I'm even aware I've made the decision.

Alone in my room, I sink down onto my bed. I spend fifteen minutes typing and deleting texts to Dani before finally settling on: *I just heard. I'm so sorry. Here if you need anything.*

I hit Send, then stare at my screen. A minute later, three bubbles pop up and I hold my breath.

Then they disappear.

I wait a few more minutes, then call Eden.

"Hi there." Eden's voice is like a purr. "Miss me already?"

I open my mouth, but nothing comes out. Suddenly, all I can think of is Mum.

"Bracha? Are you there?"

"I'm here," I manage to choke out. "I, um…do you remember my friend Dani, who works at the hostel?"

"Of course!" Eden sounds curious. "The painter."

"Right. Her grandfather passed away this morning."

"Oh?" Eden sounds less interested now. I can almost see her inspecting her nails as she listens. "That's a shame. Was it expected?"

For some reason, the question makes me flinch. "He was palliative, so…"

"So yes." Eden sighs. "Poor girl. But at least she had time to prepare."

The logical side of me knows she's right. But another part of me, a tender, bruised part I've kept hidden away for months now, is weeping. Because the truth is, you can't prepare for this kind of loss. Not emotionally. You think you can, you think you're ready, but then it happens, and somehow, it's just as much of a shock as if it had happened out of nowhere.

"The funeral is tomorrow morning," I hear myself say robotically. "I'd like to attend."

"Of course!" Eden perks up, which confuses me. "We should absolutely make an appearance and show our respect. Luckily, I just bought a new black dress a few weeks ago. It's a bit formal, but I have a nice shawl that should make it work.

Eden continues talking, but I'm not listening

anymore. I'm thinking about the art gallery, how she was there for the networking and not for the art. Sol's funeral is another social engagement for her to enjoy.

She didn't even know him, I remind myself. *She doesn't know Dani, either. Not really.*

Not like I do.

Once Eden and I make plans to meet tomorrow morning, I tell her I need to shop for something to wear as an excuse to get out of lunch. It's not that I don't want to see Eden right now.

But there's someone I want to see more.

I check my texts again. Nothing. I stand and head for the door. Then, I stop short. I don't want to go down to the lobby or the bar and be surrounded by Dani's big, swirling murals. I don't want that constant reminder that she's not here. That she's in pain.

I want to comfort her. Just as I would for Victoria, or Josh, or Katya, or Maddy, or any friend. Chewing my lip, I open the messages app and type out another text.

No need to respond. Just know I'm thinking about you.

I hit Send and wait.

Three bubbles appear for a few seconds. Then they're gone.

After a few minutes, I lay down on my bed and place my phone on my chest. I gaze at the ceiling as the hot tears build, blurring my vision. At last, I close my eyes and allow them to flow freely down my cheeks. Like I've never done before.

***

I didn't cry at Mum's funeral. There was too much to do. I remember waking up that morning with an intense tightness in my chest, and for a moment, I couldn't take a breath. The thought *we're burying her today* was like a physical weight pressing down on me. A brick on my chest.

I know how this is going to sound, but it was my to-do list that saved me. Leo and I had made it together the day before. Funerals take a lot of planning: there's the service itself, all the burial arrangements, but then there's the reception, the Shiva meal, venues, catering…it's an event. And I took on all the duties myself within twenty-four hours despite Leo, Aggie, and Dad's protests. I wanted to. For Mum, yes, but also for me. Because the longer my to-do list, the less time I had to think about the fact that she was gone.

That's the way I handle funerals.

One step at a time. Ticking off the check list.

Sol's funeral is lovely. The turnout is incredible—a hundred guests at least—and though there are plenty of tears, there's also laughter and joy. I lose count of how many of his family members step up to give a speech. It turns out Dani has two brothers, both married, each with two kids that clearly adore their quirky, artistic aunt. Dani's parents are there as well and she and her mother cling to each other during most of the service.

"He had quite a large family," Eden whispers, leaning in so our shoulders are touching. "They're very…energetic, aren't they?"

I can tell from her tone that it isn't a compliment, but I can see what she means. The Rosenbergs are that particular kind of family where everyone seems to talk all at once, raising their voices to the point of shouting. Dani's cousins, aunts, and uncles constantly interrupt one another's speeches, but none of them seem to mind and somehow they all understand each other.

"They seem like a close-knit family," I whisper back. And they do. I want to get to know them, every single one of them. Because they all know Dani in different ways than I do, I want to collect all of their stories about her and build a complete picture of her in my mind.

When Dani stands to say a few words, the raw emotion in her face jars me. Her eyes are bloodshot and shiny with tears, her nose is red, and her skin is puffy. Yet somehow, she's never looked more beautiful.

She reads a speech, and for the first time, a true hush falls over the mourners. I can't take my eyes off Dani.

"There's no right way to do this, to say everything you were, everything you mean, and everything you did," Dani says in hoarse Hebrew. "I feel so much of everything right now…"

She pauses, her gaze roaming around the room. The silence isn't just absence of sound—it's heavy, expectant, as if even the air is holding its breath. Our eyes meet briefly, and something shakes loose in my chest, a tightness I hadn't realised I was holding. Dani takes a deep breath and finishes.

"More than anything, I feel grateful."

Her words unwind in a tale of memories about her granddad as my mind replays the eulogy I read for my mother, "She filled the spaces I didn't know I had, she knew me more than I knew myself, she was there for me, without fail…"

Dani finishes with a prayer and as she heads back to her seat wiping away tears, I excuse myself, ignoring Eden's puzzled stare.

In the restroom, alone, I lock myself in a stall and sit on the toilet. I'm not hyperventilating, but it's getting close, so I lean over and put my head between my knees.

I didn't come to Israel to attend another fucking funeral.

I didn't come to Israel to experience the hardest day of my life all over again.

It's a terrible thought, a shameful thought. But it's the one my brain chooses to serve up. Seeing Dani mourn so openly, so freely, feels like a stick jabbing at a painful bruise I wasn't even aware I had.

Death is normal. Parents die. Grandparents die. It's normal. Totally normal.

But somehow, I feel that this isn't normal. I feel like the World has come to my doorstep, broken down the door, dumped all its garbage in my entrance, stayed for dinner with no offer to help with dishes, and then left, taking everything I loved with it—my brother, my mum, my life, everything I thought I knew—Dani.

By the time I return to the reception, the chairs have been pushed back and the guests are mingling around the expansive buffet table. I spot Josh and Katya chatting with Eden and feel a rush of gratitude toward my friends for keeping my date occupied.

It doesn't take long to spot Dani. She's near the end of the buffet table, staring listlessly at an impressively large bagel plate. Taking a deep breath, and pushing away my own shit, I walk over and gently nudge her elbow with mine.

"Gonna eat one? Or are you just admiring their beauty?"

Dani looks up and smiles softly. "Well, they are especially beautiful."

"Might look even better with a little shhhmear."

"Mmm. Sexy."

We both laugh a little. Then Dani looks away, and an awkward silence falls.

"That service was perfect," I say finally. "Sol would have loved it, I bet. All those stories…" I trail off because her eyes are suspiciously wet.

"Thanks," she mumbles, grabbing a napkin. "For that and just…for coming. He liked you a lot, you know. It'd mean a lot to him that you're here."

"Of course." I pause. "I'm not just here for him, though."

She stares at her napkin. We're surrounded by boisterous laughter and loud chatter, but this silence between us feels crushing.

When I can't take it anymore, I start rambling. "I've missed you. The hostel isn't the same. It's too quiet. And the magazines are always perfectly stacked. It's lonely without you in the lobby and—"

"Bracha." The way she utters my name, the thick guttural "Chet" sound, it's so pained, so broken, it stuns me back into silence. Dani crumples the napkin and tosses it on the table. "I can't deal with you right now," she whispers and walks off without looking at me.

I stare at her retreating back, wondering what the hell that was about.

"So, you gonna follow her or what?" Josh appears at my side, startling me.

"How long have you been standing there?"

"Long enough." Josh grabs a bagel and a plastic knife. "I repeat, you gonna follow her?"

"Am I supposed to?"

"Duh."

I swallow hard as he slaps the sliced bagel on a plate. "What about Eden?"

"Katya's talking her ear off," Josh says, gesturing over his shoulder with the knife. "Turns out they both read some artist's memoir they're crazy about."

He smears cream cheese on both sides of the bagel, then hands the plate to me.

"Take this bagel to Dani as a peace offering," he says solemnly, and I can't help but smile.

"Fine. Thank you."

Josh winks. "Once a wingman, always a wingman."

He slips back into the crowd before I can ask him what he means. But the thing is, I don't need to ask. I know exactly what he's implying. And it's not something I'm prepared to examine more closely right now.

This is a funeral, and I have my way of handling things. One step at a time.

I find Dani out on the balcony that overlooks the garden. She's sitting on a bench pushed back against a window, shoulders hunched, fingers pinching the bridge of her nose. When I sit next to her, she doesn't move.

"What?" she mutters.

I slide the bagel plate over her lap. "Bagel?"

For a second, I'm afraid she's going to knock the plate right out of my hands. Then her shoulders relax, and she lets out an exasperated laugh.

"Fine." She takes the top half, then starts to squash it on top of the bottom.

I clear my throat. "Hang on, you aren't gonna split it with me?"

Dani shakes her head but she's smiling as she picks up the bottom half and sets it in my open palm. I knock my half to hers like toasting champagne glasses and she laughs. We both take a bite.

I'm not sure which of us moves first. In hindsight, it was instinctive, like a reflex. But our free hands reach for one another, fingers slowly interlocking, palms pressing together.

I stare at our hands. So does Dani.

Then our eyes meet.

Her eyelashes are wet and a stray strand of auburn hair falls over her cheek. Carefully, I set my bagel down, then reach out and tuck the hair behind her ear.

Dani leans closer, just slightly. So do I. Her lips part slightly and I don't know if she's going to say something to break this spell, or if she's going to…

"Dani, come here!" A male voice yells in Hebrew.

Her hand slides out of mine. One of her brothers stands in the balcony entrance, eyeing her expectantly.

"What is it?" Dani says, setting the plate aside and getting to her feet.

"Aunt Miriam's asking for you," he replies before disappearing back inside. Dani stands there for a moment, and I hold my breath.

"See you later, Bracha," she says quietly, then follows her brother.

Before I can speak, Dani disappears inside, as she should. To be with her family.

Deflated, I turn away from the entrance and pick up the plate. Movement in my peripheral vision causes me to look up, and my stomach flips over.

The window behind the bench looks into the reception. More importantly, anyone in the reception can see out onto the balcony, and right now, it's Eden framed in the glass, wearing a glare that tells me she's been standing there long enough.

Chapter Fifteen

Eden holds my gaze for a long moment. Then she disappears from the window.

I exhale, turning back to face the garden. A moment later, the door to the balcony opens and Eden steps outside.

I keep my eyes on my lap as she slides the bagel plate over and sits. She crosses her legs, clasps her hands on her knees and clears her throat.

"So. Dani is more than just a friend from the hostel."

I feel my defence shields fly up. "No! We've never…been romantic in any way."

"Aside from holding hands and gazing into each other's eyes."

I flinch. "I meant, we haven't slept together. We've never kissed."

"But you have feelings for her." Eden doesn't pause long enough for me to respond, which is for the best, as I'm more than a little terrified as to what I might say. "You had no intention of inviting me today, did you? When you called, you said *I'd like to attend.* I merely assumed you wanted me to come as your date."

I stay silent because she's not wrong.

"So perhaps I share a bit of the blame here." Eden sighs, glancing at the window behind us. "Funerals bring out strong emotions. You are a rational woman, Bracha. I'm sure in any other circumstance, you would have immediately seen how this looked."

Now I'm lost. "How what looked?"

Eden gestures to the bagel plate between us. "You, leaving your date to sit with another woman, holding hands and—let's be honest, Bracha—kissing. Because that's what would have happened had Dani's brother not interrupted. You would have kissed another woman in plain view of everyone at this reception while I stood there looking like a complete fool."

My mouth opens and closes. Again, I have no words. It's like my brain is playing catch up, slowly decoding the real meaning of her words as one thing is becoming crystal clear.

Eden isn't angry that I nearly kissed someone else. She's angry that I nearly made her look bad in front of other people.

I wrote down a list of what my ideal wife would look like on a piece of paper. With Eden, our entire relationship would be defined precisely like that: on paper. So long as it appeared happy and loving, that was all that mattered. *You love who you love*, Dani told me on the beach, *even when it doesn't make sense on paper*.

"Now, we've got that out of the way," Eden continues briskly. "On to the next step. I forgive you, Bracha. But you must promise never to embarrass me like that again."

At last, I meet her eyes. Beautiful, clear, and so cold. How had I never seen it before? My future with Eden flashes through my mind. A marriage that ticked

170

every point on the list, a marriage of logic and reason, but with compromise. A marriage without any real emotion. Without passion. Without love.

I take a deep breath.

"Eden, I'm sorry. Truly. But this…" I gesture between us. "This isn't going to work for me."

Eden blinks. "This…meaning our relationship?"

"Yes."

"You're breaking up with me?"

I take another deep breath.

When I speak, my voice is firm. "Yes."

She stares at me for a moment that seems to drag on forever. The more seconds that pass, the more I start to worry. Will she cry? Try to rationalise me out of my decision? Make a scene in front of Dani's family?

Finally, Eden shrugs.

"It's just as well. I wasn't looking forward to dealing with all your family drama, anyway. Too much hassle."

She gets to her feet, straightens out her black dress, and nods.

"Goodbye, Bracha."

"Bye," I manage to choke out as she strides back inside. The door snaps closed behind her, and that's it. Eden is gone.

***

I slip out of the reception hall unnoticed and begin the long walk back to Beit Yam.

Breakups are supposed to hurt. They're supposed to upset you, make you sad, angry, desperate. In some cases, breakups can even make you grieve. It's the death of a relationship.

All I feel right now is relief.

Eden was technically perfect. But I can't deny the truth anymore: I didn't love her and she didn't love me. A marriage at what cost? To feel more alone? Because now, I realise there's someone who makes me feel like I'm not alone.

I know it is said that there is someone for everyone, but honestly, I hadn't believed that for years. I believed love was something left to the hormones of teenagers, the whims of adolescents, love was ad hoc, disruptive, spontaneous, irrational. I focussed on more practical matters. It made sense to me: focus on studying, building a career, and enjoying relationships on my terms—never at the expense of stability. But now, I think I get *it*.

A few blocks before the hostel, I step into an empty alley and pull out my phone.

The call rings once, twice, three times. I'm mentally rehearsing what I'll say when it goes to voice mail, but then:

"Hey."

The sound of Maddy's voice causes a wave of homesickness that causes me to lean against the brick wall.

"Wow. You picked up."

"I did." Maddy sighs. "I've been meaning to text you back, I just…I don't know."

"It's okay," I say. "You were pissed."

"I'm still pissed, Bracha."

"Right." I brace myself to say what I need to say. "And I didn't understand why. But I think now I do. I led you on, Maddy. I honestly didn't realise that's what I was doing but that's no excuse for hurting you. And…I'm sorry."

I hold my breath as the silence stretches out.

"Thank you," she says finally.

"And I want you to know I love you," I add.

Maddy sighs. "I love you too, Bracha. Even if you are a jerk sometimes."

I smile. "Thanks."

"So, how's the wife hunt going?" Her tone is teasing, but there's still a little bite to her words.

Now it's my turn to fall silent. I stare at the fire escape against the opposite wall, my throat tightening.

"Bracha?"

"Not great," I tell her. "Turns out making that list maybe wasn't the best idea."

"Shocking." Maddy pauses. "You okay?"

"I will be."

We chat for a few more minutes before closing with plans to catch up when I am back. I am relieved and sad at the same time that Maddy, one of my best friends, was in love with me and never told me. I can't make that mistake.

I spend the next few days holed up at the hostel. Aside from hanging out with Josh and Katya at the bar a few times, I'm pretty much in a self-imposed solitary confinement. My phone lights up with messages from Dad and Eli asking questions about the house, along with photos from Leo and Aggie showing all the improvements they've made. I don't feel anger or resentment. I don't feel anything at all.

I find a few flights home next week. It's not like I'm about to start up the wife search again. Even with a month and a half left on my visa, the thought of going on more dates turns my stomach. So, I have no reason to stay.

Still, I don't buy a ticket. Not yet.

Dani doesn't return to work. By the third day, I'm starting to worry she's quit altogether, although Omer assures me, she hasn't.

So, I take over for Dani, tidying and organising behind the front desk, doing the linen laundry, cleaning the little kitchen, and checking guests in. Katya enters the lobby one afternoon to find me on my hands and knees, scrubbing the floorboards with a soapy sponge.

"I hope Omer is paying you for this," she says lightly, grabbing a magazine from the stack on the desk.

"Nope." I straighten up and stretch out my lower back. "Just trying to make things easier for Dani when she gets back. She's taking a lot of time for mourning; I know this must be difficult for her."

"Bracha, love." Katya waits until I look at her. Her eyes are soft and filled with compassion. "I don't think the reason Dani hasn't come back to work is because she's mourning her grandfather."

I swallow hard. "What do you mean?"

Katya rolls up the magazine and bops me gently on the head. "I mean, of course, she misses her grandfather, but I think not coming back to work has a lot more to do with you. If you want to see Dani, you're going to have to take the initiative."

She leans over to kiss me on the cheek, then disappears down the hall.

I sit on the floor, back against the wall and toss down the sponge. For a few minutes, I agonise over the wording of my texts. Then I hit call instead and close my eyes as it rings.

"Allo?" Dani's Hebrew pops through my phone.

"Dani, it's Bracha." I can feel my heart thudding against my ribs. "I really need to talk to you. Can you meet me at the beach?"

Dani doesn't respond at first. I wait it out, counting my heartbeats.

"Okay," she says, sounding distant. "I can be there in half an hour."

***

We meet at Sol's Spot.

Dani's wrapped in a navy-blue oversized jacket, her auburn hair tumbling loose down her back. She smiles a little sadly when she sees me.

"Hi," I say.

"Hi."

Dani's Hebrew is soft, absent of the usual pep in her voice.

Together, we face the sea. It's overcast today, a

crisp chill in the breeze—not freezing by any means but sharp enough to keep the swimmers away.

"Your family seems lovely," I say at last, still a little lost for words.

"I hope everything is going okay at home."

The corner of Dani's mouth quirks up. "Sol would never have let us mope around Bracha."

"Of course not…" I hesitate. There's more I want to say—about the garden, about that moment at the funeral we both seem too afraid to name—but the words knot in my throat. Instead, I shift.

"I wish you had told the story of the time you finally swam in the ocean."

"What? You know I've never done that. Water phobic over here, remember?"

I nod. "I remember, yeah. I remember you telling me how you used to watch Sol swim out there. How powerful he looked. He wanted you to come out in the waves, didn't he? I think he'd love that story."

She's still staring at me like I've lost my mind. So, I pull a piece of paper from my pocket, unfold it, and hold it up.

She frowns. "Is that the nine-point woman list?"

"Yeah." I glance out at the grey sea. "I'm going to rip it up. But only if you take a swim with me."

Dani's eyes widen. "Are you serious?"

"Yup."

"You're really abandoning your quest for perfection?"

"Technically yes, figuratively no."

"Well then." Dani crosses her arms and smiles.

"You should rip that list up for your own good, not part of some bargain."

I consider this. "You're right," I say, and her mouth is now in a full smile as I tear the list to shreds.

I throw the pieces into the air. Then I shoot Dani a grin before pulling off my shoes one by one, falling over myself as I sprint into the sea. The frigid saltwater laps at my calves, and I let out a delighted shriek. Once the waves are at my waist, I dive into them.

With my eyes squeezed closed, I blow out a stream of bubbles and start to pump my legs. Instantly, I remember why swimming in the ocean is far superior than any pool. The way the current finds me, wraps around me, and pulls me out deeper and deeper, as if it's guiding me home.

At last, when I can't bear the ache in my lungs anymore, I pull myself up to the surface. I'm gasping for air, laughing, disoriented, and when it occurs to me that I'm going to have to walk back to the hostel in sopping wet clothes, I laugh even harder.

"You're crazy."

Turning, I see Dani standing not far from me. The waves lap at her ankles and she lets out a nervous laugh as she takes another step, then another. I move toward her, soaking wet, and hold out my hands. Our fingers interlock and I pull her out towards me until the water reaches her knees.

Dani squeezes my hands and stops. "That's far enough for now," she whispers. Her hazel eyes sparkle with exhilaration and fear and too many other emotions for me to identify.

"For now," I say softly, and we stay just like that for a long time.

***

Back at the hostel, I take a long, hot shower. When I emerge in a fresh pair of jeans and a sweater, I feel like a new person.

I hear Omer's booming voice before I enter the lobby. He's chatting with a couple of backpackers while Dani sits behind the counter, scribbling furiously. When she sees me, she quickly folds up the paper.

"Please let us know if you need anything!" Omer calls after the backpackers as they traipse down the hall. Then he heaves an enormous sigh and turns to Dani. "Is there anything I can do to change your mind? Anything at all?"

I frown, glancing from Omer to Dani. "Change your mind about what?"

Dani's cheeks darken. "Nothing."

"Nothing?" Omer throws his hands up. "My favourite employee has resigned. That isn't nothing. Although I'm thrilled for you, of course. *Thrilled*."

He plants a kiss on Dani's cheek then lets out an exaggerated sob as he retreats into the office.

I stare at Dani, but she doesn't meet my gaze.

"You resigned? Why?"

Dani chews her lip. "I'm moving to New York."

The words knock the wind out of me "Because of

Riley?" I blurt out.

She turns the folded paper over and over in her hands. "Because I was offered an art scholarship at NYU," she says finally. "I applied months ago. It was a long shot, I didn't think I'd get it…but, well. I got it."

"Oh. I didn't know…" I struggle to process this, my eyes flicking over to the murals on the wall.

Dani catches me looking and raises an eyebrow. "You didn't know what? That art was more than a hobby to me?"

I feel a flash of guilt, followed by defensiveness. "That's not what I said. You did tell me you wanted to pursue a career in art."

"I did. And you assumed I would fail."

She's right, though it pains me to admit it. I cast around for a way to redirect the conversation.

"So, is Riley excited? Guess she doesn't have to plan any more trips to Israel she doesn't intend on taking."

It's a low blow and I regret the words immediately. But desperation is choking me, making me panic. I don't want Dani to go to New York and I can't even fully explain why, not even to myself. Not right now.

Dani looks up, eyes flashing with indignation. "You're right, Bracha. She doesn't. Long distance doesn't work, right? Not even with someone you really love?"

She's taunting me, rubbing her supposedly perfect relationship in my face.

"She's sleeping with her boss." I can't stop myself

now. The words pour out. "And I think you know that, Dani. Those business trips over the holidays? It's such a lame excuse. And it won't stop just because you're there. You deserve better than that. You—"

"Stop." Dani tosses the paper down and glares at me. "Thanks for the advice. Anything else you want to say?"

I open my mouth. Yes, there's more I want to say. But the words are clogged in my throat. Dani gives me a long moment, waiting, then shakes her head and disappears into the office.

I run my hands over my still-wet hair. What was I thinking? Why did I say all of that?

Why didn't I say what I knew, deep down, I wanted to say?

My eyes fall on the folded piece of paper. I pick it up and open it.

The perfectly imperfect girlfriend…
Doesn't take sugar
Eats at precisely 8, noon, 4 and 8
Brilliantly logical
Emotionally immature
Total time waster
Never tires of stacking magazines, no matter how messy they may get
Possibly OCD
Beautiful

My mouth goes dry. This is what Dani was writing after our swim in the ocean. A list of qualities that her "perfectly imperfect girlfriend" possesses.

A list of *my* qualities.

I swallow hard. Then I fold the list up into the tiniest possible square, shove it in my pocket, head to the office door to knock, and stop short, before turning around and heading up to my room.

Chapter Sixteen

Almost a week passes. Every morning, I wake up and search for flights to Sydney. I find dozens.

I leave the tabs open, tickets unpurchased.

I spend my days wandering the streets of Tel Aviv, occasionally meandering into a bookshop or gallery. Josh presses me to join him at the clubs at night but eventually gives up when I refuse. Katya brings me black coffee from The Galya because I can't bring myself to walk inside, but their espresso is far superior to the hostel's coffeemaker.

I reply to texts from my family. Short, courteous responses that won't invite questions but are enough to keep them from worrying.

Saturday morning at just after six, a sharp knocking at my door jars me awake.

"Hang on," I mumble, throwing off the blanket. I open the door to find Katya standing there, dusty duffel bag at her feet, her face streaked with tears. Instantly, I'm wide awake. "What's wrong?"

Her voice is raspy. "I'm going to India."

"Um. Okay." I rub my eyes. "Why?"

"You know I've been planning this trip forever."

"Why *now*?"

"I just…" Katya shakes her head and pinches the bridge of her nose. "I had a fight with Josh last night."

I step back and wave for her to come inside. She does, dragging her duffel along with her. Once we're seated side by side on the bed, Katya takes a deep breath.

"It was supposed to be a fling," she says at last. "I mean, neither of us said so, but we both knew that's all it was. Except after New Year's, I just…started to have deeper feelings for him."

I put an arm around her. "And you told him?"

Katya lets out a humourless laugh. "No! I didn't because I knew he'd run away. Then, last night, we're having drinks because he finally found a job translating, and I'm telling him how proud I am of him, and suddenly he blurts out that he loves me."

My mouth falls open. "Josh said he *loves* you?"

"Yeah." Katya tilts her head back and sighs. "And did I say it back? No. Instead, I freaked out. I said I thought you didn't do commitment. And he said maybe people can change. And I said sure, but can *you*? Can you actually be monogamous? Do you *want* that? And he got all defensive and said do you *want* to go to India? Because you've been talking about it forever, and you're still here, and I think you're full of shit about it. And I said, yeah, I'm going to India now, actually, and if you really love me, maybe you should come. And he said show me the ticket and I threw my drink at him and left. Then I bought a fucking ticket because, you know, to prove him wrong."

By the time she finishes, she is almost laughing, hopelessly.

I exhale slowly. "That's not the worst argument."

"I suppose."

"He said he loves you…"

Katya's phone buzzes, and she glances at the screen. "My ride's here."

My heart twists a little as she stands. I get to my feet and pull her into a hug.

"I'm going to miss you," I say quietly.

"Don't start getting all sentimental now, Bracha Cohen," she says, pulling away and giving me a playful shove. "You'll keep in touch, right? Let me know how things turn out back in Australia? When you eventually get there." She gives me a nudge.

"Of course." I nudge back.

We smile at one another, and I'm startled to realise tears are filling my eyes. Lightning quick, Katya plants a kiss on my cheek.

"Bye, Bracha," she says, and then she's gone.

I sit heavily on my bed, feeling drained. Slowly, I lie down and pull the blanket back over my legs. But just as I'm drifting back to sleep, a buzzing on my phone brings me back to reality.

My phone vibrates again, and I snatch it up, irritated. "What?"

"Bracha?" Josh practically barks my name. "Do you know where Katya is?"

Groaning, I sit up again. "On her way to the airport."

"What?"

"She's going to India." I pause for a long yawn. "And you're an idiot. But a brave idiot."

"I know. I know I am. Thanks. I didn't think she'd…" Josh sounds panicked now. "She told you what happened?"

"Yeah."

"I don't know what's wrong with me," Josh says. "I mean, I do—commitment scares the shit out of me—but I meant it. I love her. I got this job. I thought she'd want to stay. Because I want to…you know. Do the thing."

Despite my exhaustion, I laugh. "Do the thing?"

"Yeah. Shut up, you know what I mean." Josh lets out a frustrated sort of growl. "But come on. I put myself out there last night and told her how I felt and what's her response? *Then come to India with me.* I mean, doesn't she get how hard it was for me to even say that? Why am I supposed to follow her, anyway? If *she* loves *me,* why not stay here? Why—"

"Josh," I interrupt loudly. "I say this with love: can you do the job from India?"

He's silent for a second. "What?"

"Translating? Can you do it online or put it off? You love her, right?"

"Yeah."

"So, can you?"

"Well, maybe."

"Then what are you doing?"

This time, the silence is so long, I start to think he's hung up.

"You're right," he says finally. "Yeah. You're right. I need to get to the airport."

***

Twenty minutes later, I meet Josh in the lobby. His

eyes have that red-rimmed, slightly wild look that tells me he didn't sleep at all last night. He wreaks of cigarettes and his beard is more than a five o'clock shadow. He blinks when he sees me, like I'm a mirage.

"You're coming?" he asks.

I shrug. "You know me. I can't resist the sappy 'chase the girl through the airport' scene in every romance movie ever."

A grin flickers over Josh's face as he orders a taxi. "That's you. Bracha Cohen, die hard romantic." He says sarcastically.

Once we're in the backseat, Josh can't stop fidgeting. He checks his phone, his seatbelt, his window, his wallet. He shows me his virtual boarding pass to New Delhi. Same flight as Katya."

"I can't believe you're both leaving," I say, mostly to distract him. "The hostel won't be the same without you."

"Aren't you heading back to Australia soon, though?" Josh asks. "Or is there a reason you're hanging around?"

I sigh. "No. No reason at all."

We're quiet for a moment. Then Josh turns to face me. "Come on, Bracha. Out with it. What happened with Dani?"

I open my mouth to say *nothing, none of your business, I don't want to talk about it.* But instead, it all pours out: our moment at Sol's funeral, tearing up the list at the beach, standing in the ocean together, Dani telling me she's moving to New York, all the dumb stuff I said and finally, her list.

"Damn," Josh says when I finish. "Hypocrite much?"

I frown. "I don't think she's a hypocrite, just—"

"Not Dani, you!" Josh shoves my shoulder. "You're as much of an idiot as I am."

"I'm sorry?"

Josh rolls his eyes. "Fine. You gave me some tough love this morning, so I owe you. Here's the deal: when Dani said that thing about long-distance relationships, she wasn't rubbing her and Riley in your face. She was testing the waters to see if you still felt that way. Or if you'd be open to, say, a relationship with someone in New York. Like a long-distance relationship with her."

I open my mouth to argue, but Josh holds up his hand.

"You ripped up your perfect woman list. Cool. Dani makes an imperfect woman list and it's all about you. She tells you about New York, gives you an opening. And you fucked it up."

I stare at the buildings whizzing past outside my window, my mind whirling. "But she's still with Riley."

"Is she?" Josh says. "Because she told you she's moving because she got a scholarship to NYU. She didn't say a word about a girlfriend."

He falls silent as the airport comes into view. I'm quiet, too, turning over in my mind everything Josh has said.

The second the car pulls to a stop, Josh flies out the door. I give the driver a quick "thanks" before sprinting after him.

As we race through the terminal, hysterical laughter bubbles in my throat. *This is such a cliché!* I want to say, but I don't have the breath.

"Last call to board flight EY473 to New Delhi…"

"Wait!" Josh yells, picking up speed. "*Katya!*"

The laughter bursts out of me, and I have to slow down. It's all too much; the running, the desperate cry…*all that's missing is rain*, I think, and that only makes me laugh harder.

But when I reach the gate just in time to see Katya throw herself into Josh's arms, the laughter dies in my throat.

I slow to a halt and stare, along with everyone else at the next gate over, as Josh pulls the rubber band from his hair.

Then he drops to one knee.

"Oh my god, Josh," I whisper.

Katya claps both hands over her mouth as Josh starts to speak. With all the terminal noise, I can't make out his words. But I don't have to.

"*Yes!*" Katya cries, kneeling down and throwing her arms around Josh. They cling to each other as the entire gate bursts into applause. When they pull apart, Josh carefully wraps the rubber band a few times around Katya's ring finger. I can't stop staring at the smile on his face. It's hard to explain, but it's almost like this is the first time I've seen him really, truly smile. The first time I've seen him purely happy.

He helps Katya to her feet, and she plants a kiss on his lips. Then she spots me, and her face lights up.

"We're engaged!" she cries, holding out the hand

with the rubber band.

Laughing, I walk over to give them each a hug. "Congratulations," I say, glancing at Josh. "That was absolutely ridiculous, by the way," I say to Josh. "Katya could lose her finger."

A little voice in my head whispers, *I want that ridiculous kind of love.*

"Are you two boarding?" A flight attendant clearly unimpressed asks.

"Yes!" Josh picks up his bag and grabs Katya's hand. "Let's do this."

Katya turns to me, eyes shining. "I saw Dani at check-in."

My heart stutters. "What?"

"She might still be here. She was going to her gate. I don't know which; check the board!" Katya allows Josh to tug her toward the flight attendant. "Bye, Bracha! Good luck!"

I watch as the attendant closes the doors behind them.

Then I turn and sprint for the nearest departures board. There are plenty of flights to New York today, including both JFK and LaGuardia airports. I skim the gate numbers for the next few flights before I take off again.

I pass gate after gate, slowing just enough to scan the faces of the travellers milling around or sitting and staring at their phones. My pulse is racing as I picture Josh falling to his knee like that. What will I do, when I find Dani?

But before long, it becomes obvious that the

universe isn't willing to dole out a second over-the-top romantic airport moment today. There are simply too many gates and too many people.

At last, I come to a stop in front of a massive window and try to catch my breath. For a few minutes, I watch as planes slowly queue on the runway and take off one by one.

Eventually, I give up.

I wander back through the terminal. This time, instead of focusing on faces, I look at the walls. I look at the mural of Israel's history, documenting scientific discoveries, medical advances, but also tales of war and freedom, heartache. There's the Goldstar beer display, a full twenty meters of illuminated bottles of the local beverage of choice on warm summer days. The glow forms a halo around each golden bottle, an illusion of the brand's god-like stature. Next to that display, in contrast, is the forest green advertisement for Maccabee, Israel's second most popular beer— that's made by the same company.

I suddenly remember an old joke my dad used to tell about the Jewish man stranded on a desert island for twenty years.

"When he was finally rescued, he was asked why he built two temples," Dad would say, eyes already twinkling with the punchline. "He said, this one I pray in every Saturday. That one, I wouldn't set foot in!"

Jewish culture is emboldened by a good argument. When it comes to beer and temples, I respect both.

The exit comes into view. I remember with agonising clarity how I felt marching through those doors two months ago. I was here, determined to find the perfect wife, so sure of what I wanted. I hardly remembered any Hebrew, but I carried happy memories of speaking it, of connecting with others. I ran away from my problems at home, but they followed me here. I walked out of that exit and ended up at a hostel where I met someone who made me happy. Who reconnected me, with *myself*.

And then I lost her.

I slow to a halt in front of another giant board of Arrivals and Departures and stare at the countless flights on the screen.

With a heavy sigh, I pull out my wallet and head for the El Al desk. The attendant smiles as I approach.

"How can I help you?" she asks.

I force a smile back.

"Next available flight to Sydney, please."

Chapter Seventeen

Honeymoon in Phuket! Appropriate much.

Half a dozen laughing emojis follow Katya's caption. I smile wistfully at the photo of her and Josh on a white beach, beaming against a backdrop of impossibly aqua waters lapping against massive, moss-covered boulders. Josh's hair is still loose, and the smile on his face is pure contentment. I spot the rubber band twisted around Katya's finger, although now there's a definite glint of gold there as well.

"Who's the happy couple?"

I glance up to see Victoria peering over my shoulder. "Just some friends I met in Tel Aviv. They ended up eloping to India."

"How spontaneous. I love it." Victoria squints at me. "You okay, honey?"

"Yes. Why?"

Victoria shrugs and heads over to the coffeemaker. "You've been back for almost a week and I have yet to see you crack a smile."

She glances up and laughs as I paste on the most fake smile I can manage.

"Fine, fine." Victoria adds milk to her mug. "Just kind of seems like you've been on auto-pilot. When I come back from vacation, I can't wait to get back to work. But that was a long trip, huh? I guess it'll take time to get back into the swing of things."

"Yeah." I stare down at my screen. *Auto-pilot*

about sums it up. I slipped back into my old routine as soon as I got back: morning runs, long work days, unwinding in the kitchen in the evening while Aggie bustles about making dinner, late-night chats with Leo. I haven't seen Dad yet, though we've texted a few times. Thankfully, he hasn't pressed me once about reaching out to Eli.

Because I haven't. Not yet.

I'm waiting for the post-vacation fog to lift, except it's gotten heavier with each passing day. I finish my morning runs covered in sweat, but I don't feel the same rush of endorphins that I used to. Leo's attempts to convince me into going for a drink or a movie are easy to deflect. It doesn't help that he's about to leave on a long business trip. Soon I won't even have him around.

It takes a few seconds for me to realise my thumb has been flipping through more posts. When I stop, my breath hitches in my chest.

Dani stands in front of a white column. She's pointing up at the massive purple and white NYU flag hanging over her head. Her eyes are wide with comical shock, her mouth open in disbelief. The caption simply reads: *I DID IT.*

I won't deny that I've checked her feed more than a few times since I got home—a few hundred times. I'd actually given up hope that she would ever post again. Yet here she is, living her dream, pursuing a degree in art.

And here I am.

"Doctor Cohen, you're needed in resus."

The voice over the loudspeaker shakes me from my angst. Without giving myself too much time to think about it, I hit *like* on Dani's post. Then I shove my phone in my pocket and get back to work.

Two motorbike accidents, a dislocated shoulder and one drug overdose later, I'm off. My brain is so zoned out that I don't see the figure sitting hunched on the front steps until I slam the car door closed.

The figure's head snaps up and I freeze.

"Hey, sis," Eli says.

I drop my keys.

The last time I actually saw my brother was the day he was arrested. He'd just come off a bender, hair long and stringy, scruff on his chin, shirt sleeves rolled up to show the tattoos winding around his biceps, jeans in such bad need of a wash that they looked brown. At well over six feet tall, Eli could look scary when he wanted to. But when he was looking for his next fix? He is downright terrifying.

But now, as he gets to his feet, I reluctantly have to acknowledge that Aggie was right. Eli really cleaned up—well, he cleaned up his looks, at least. He must have had a few buzz cuts in prison because now a thick layer of dark fuzz covers his head. His face is freshly shaven, and his flannel shirt and jeans are clean. This is the Eliyahu that had all the girls at school throwing themselves at his feet.

I scoop up my keys, trying to hide my embarrassment. "What are you doing?"

Eli sticks his hands in his pockets as I walk toward him. "Waiting for you to get home."

"You have a key, don't you?" I snap. "Why not let yourself in? Again?"

A shrug. "Politeness."

I brush past him and unlock the front door. Inside, I dump my bag on the floor and head straight for the couch. Eli follows me inside, closing the door as I flop back on the couch and stare at the ceiling.

"Rough day at work?" he asks, dropping his satchel by his feet.

"It's emergency," I reply shortly. "It's always a rough day."

"Yeah." Eli hovers at the end of the couch. I do my best to ignore him but just the sight of my brother in the living room sparks hot anger in my chest.

Our conversation standoff barely lasts a minute.

"So…here." Eli tosses a Post-it note on my stomach.

Gritting my teeth, I snatch it up. "*Wallpaper mould in master bedroom, cracked pipe downstairs bathroom*…what's this?"

"The stuff that still needs fixing." Eli sits on the arm of the couch. "Dad and I knocked a bunch of tasks off the list while you were away. This is all that's left."

I pinch the Post-it between my fingers like it's a soiled napkin and drop it on the floor.

With a barely audible sigh, Eli picks it up. "I took a week off when I heard you were back. I'd like to get back to work Monday before these issues get worse."

I'm not buying this nice guy act. "Cool. Hey, who's paying for all this? The materials, the tools…"

Eli clears his throat. "Yeah, so I've been keeping a tab for everything. I was thinking maybe we could split it fifty-fifty, since the house is split between us."

I mock laugh. "Figures you'd assume that without actually running it by me first. But then again, it's always about money with you."

"That's not true." The defensiveness in his tone gives me a deep sense of satisfaction.

I sit up and clasp my hands in my lap. "Fuck it. Let's just sell the house and split our inheritance in cash. That's why you're really here, right? Playing repairman, pretending like you actually give a shit about this place…"

Anger flashes in his eyes. "Sell it? I don't want to sell Mum's house, Bracha. All the memories we have here, I—"

"What memories?" I exclaim, red-hot anger washing over me. "You were hardly ever here and when you were, you were smacked out of your mind! Do you even remember the last time you saw Mum? Do you remember how she sobbed? Do you have any fucking clue what she was like after you got arrested? It destroyed her, Eli. *You* destroyed her."

I'm breathing heavily, fists clenched. At some point, I stood up without even realising it and now I'm glaring up at my brother. I've never been scared of his height nor his anger when he was riled up. I wait for him to dismiss my words, to hurl hurtful accusations right back at me, maybe even pin me against the wall so I can fight back harder.

Instead, I'm shocked to see tears glistening in his

eyes.

"I know." His voice is thick with emotion. "I know, Bracha. Because after that, I had six months of sobriety and cement walls to think about it. To beat myself up. To hate myself. To forgive myself. And to grieve. Which I'm kind of thinking you still haven't done."

I stare at him in disbelief. "Excuse me? I was at the funeral, Eli. I planned the thing."

"Yeah, but you haven't grieved." His tone is so calm, so certain, that I want to scream. Since when is Eli the face of calm.

"You ran away instead. And hey, I get it," Eli pauses, "No judgement sis. But now you're back and you're like a zombie. That's not me talking, that's everyone else. They're worried you're depressed."

I start to ask who *everyone else* is, then stop short. The idea of Eli talking about my "depression" with Dad, Leo, or Aggie is too infuriating for words. "Maybe I'm depressed because I knew you'd be back to leech off me."

"That's not why I'm here." Eli closes his eyes briefly. "Mum's death affected me too, Bracha. I fucked up but I'm not heartless. Even before she…passed, I was trying. I paid her back some of what I owed her."

"Sure you did."

Eli studies me for a moment. Then he picks up his satchel and pulls out a notebook. "I've been wanting to show you this. Can we just sit down? Just for a minute?"

This isn't the Eli I'm used to. Even before his drug problems, he was always ready for a heated argument. This calmness is a thousand times more irritating but if he isn't going to yell, I'm not going to, either. So, I sit down, shifting away when he sits next to me.

Eli places his hands on the notebook cover. "You aren't allowed many belongings in prison," he says slowly. "No wallet, no phone, all that gets locked up. But books and journals are okay."

"You kept a journal?" I can't keep the incredulity out of my voice.

He shakes his head. "This isn't mine. It was Mum's."

He slides the book onto my lap. I stare at it as if it's a massive wall, waiting to be torn down. But not by me. I can't.

Sighing, Eli opens to the first page. I'm expecting journal entries in Mum's perfect strokes. Instead, I find myself staring at a sketch of what is unmistakably Aunt Aggie with wings. Beneath are the words *My Angel*.

"What is this?" I whisper.

Eli swallows hard. "A few months before I was arrested, I came over while you were at work and found Mum lying in bed. I could smell vodka. It was well before noon. I wanted to call a doctor, you, but she wouldn't let me. She said she was having a bad day."

My throat starts to feel swollen. I'd never spoken to Mum about those days, but I was aware of them. One day she'd be fine, happy, joyful. The next morning, it was as if all the energy had been drained from her body, and she resorted to self-medicating. Those days were the hardest for all of us.

"I told her I had them, too," Eli says quietly. "Those days were the worst for me, because I know exactly what will make me feel better. Well, temporarily. Those are the days where I feel like it's either get high or die."

I press my lips together, staring at the portrait of Aggie. I flip to the next page and see a teenage Eli drawn in various shades of yellows and browns. *The Golden Boy* is written in a familiar cursive beneath his feet.

"Mum told me it's good to have something to help." Eli lets out a small laugh. "But that whatever it is should be legal. Like drawing. That's what she would do, or at least tried to do before, well, you know…" He trails off and puts his hand over the scarring on his left arm that's formed from track marks.

I know what I'm going to see on the next page before I turn it and now, I'm staring at Mum's drawing of me, my hair wild as if I'm standing in a strong wind, my eyes narrowed and fierce, my mouth stretched in a grim smile. A single word is scribbled below me: *Lioness.*

The image blurs and I squeeze my eyes closed, I thought I'd forgotten. All of us together playing dress up for Purim, Dad joking around as an ape because of the sheer amount of dark hair all over his chest. We'd agreed on a jungle theme that year, the year before we left Israel. Mum dressed as the skinniest elephant known to humankind but with gloriously large ears made from grey socks. Eli painted delicate whiskers on his face then wrapped mum's leopard print scarf around his neck. "The cheekiest of leopards," he exclaimed. The memory forces more tears to swell up behind my eyes and I try to shake it off—not wanting to cry in front of my brother.

"It's always stayed with me that memory of us," Eli says interjecting my thoughts, "You got so upset when Dad suggested you looked like a monkey with that homemade lion suit."

"I'm not a monkey, I'm a lion!" I choke out. Remembering the hurt I felt clutching that scrappy mane like it was my crown, determined to defend my identity.

Eli laughs, the kind of laugh that warms the edges of a memory, and for a moment, I feel closer to him.

He takes the book from my lap flipping through to the back.

"She always loved to draw, she just didn't get the time at work," Eli says as he turns the page to a sketch of mum that somehow looks familiar.

She's sitting cross-legged, head bowed as if in prayer. She used every shade of blue imaginable. Teal blue crossed with navy in her long hair. Her face filled with a slate blue down to her neck. But the darkest blue is in the shadows beneath her eyes. Tired eyes. I remember this version of mum, it's the version I tried to change so much.

I understand what Eli's trying to tell me. That Mum's struggle with depression began long before his struggle with addiction. That life back in Australia wasn't easy like her and Dad thought it would be. My heart aches, that I wasn't enough to help her cope.

"Anyway, Mum told me she wanted to go back to Israel," Eli continues. "She was having all these issues with the house, she was overwhelmed…and she couldn't afford it. I paid for her flight."

I picture the unused plane ticket and feel something click in my jaw. All this time, I was here for Mum when Eli was off getting in trouble. How is it he knew a part of her that I never did?

"It was kind of a payback," Eli adds. "That ticket. Because she paid for me to go to rehab."

Finally, I look up at him. "You went to rehab?"

He nods. "And I got a job. Construction contractor said he'd give me a chance. I was trying to clean up, Bracha. Mum was going to Israel, I was on the straight and narrow, everything was going great…but then she skipped her flight, and that's when she took a turn for the worse, and I relapsed." Eli grimaces. "Badly. You know the rest."

I look at my brother for a long moment. Imagining him blaming himself in prison. Having nowhere to run and hide, like I did. For the first time in ages, the resentment I feel toward him starts to subside. A deep, long-repressed sadness bubbles up instead, and I allow the sob to rise up in my throat.

"I miss her," I manage to gasp before sobbing into my hands.

Eli waits a few seconds, then gently puts his arm around my shoulder. I don't lean into him. But I don't push him away, either. We sit there for I don't know how many minutes as I finally release all the grief I've kept bottled up for months.

He pulls away when the back door slams. "Yoohoo! Bracha?" Aggie calls in her sing-song voice. "How does lentil curry sound for dinner? I bought a beautiful bag of fresh lentils and picked some fresh chili from the garden this afternoon!"

Eli gives me a sidelong glance. "I'll take off," he whispers, starting to stand. But I put my hand on his arm, and he falls still.

I'm exhausted. My eyes and throat are still aching and my limbs feel like they're made of stone. Thoughts—things I want to say—swirl curiously in my mind, as if maybe Eli holds the answers. As if the weight of grief I've been carrying is a burden he's been sharing too.

"Stay for dinner?" I say hoarsely. Feeling an easement between us.

Eli's shoulders relax, he places Mum's journal in his satchel and smiles. "Sure."

Chapter Eighteen

Over the weekend, Aggie, Leo and I finish going through all of Mum's things. As we sort and organise things into categories of "keep" or "donate," we reminisce about Mum. For the first time, it isn't painful. In fact, talking about her makes me feel almost comforted, even if with a big sense of sadness and a whole lot of crying.

"I think what made it so hard is that I thought I should have been able to save her," I say, folding a white silk blouse between sobs.

Leo and Aggie fall still, eyes wide.

"How do you mean, Bracha?" Leo asks hesitantly.

I shrug, adding a pair of black pumps to the donations box. "I'm a doctor. Mum was sick."

Aggie looks mildly horrified. "Bracha, that's…no…that's simply not true. Your mother never would have expected that of you—none of us would have!"

"I know that now," I tell her as I wipe my snotty nose, and Leo reaches out to squeeze my shoulder. "It just took me a while to figure it out."

"For someone so smart, you're often quite slow on the uptake," Leo tells me with a teasing smile.

I briefly think of Dani, then push her from my mind. "You're not wrong," I reply.

Monday morning, Dad and Eli arrive bright and early dressed in overalls and loaded with paint tins, brushes, and all sorts of tools. A father and son team I didn't think could exist again.

"Will this place still be standing when I get home from work?" I ask mildly, holding a steaming cup of coffee as Dad begins mixing paint in the garage.

"Not to worry," he tells me. "We're going to start on the basics, then hire professionals when needed." Dad pauses, glancing through the garage entrance into the house to make sure Eli is out of earshot. "And I'll be here the whole time. Keeping an eye on things, make sure we stay on course. Eli made a list." He starts to pat his pockets, then frowns. "Eli?"

"Yeah?" Eli pokes his head in the kitchen.

"Do you have the list?"

Eli shrugs. "Don't need it. I remember everything that needs to be done. It was just a guide."

I take in his tool belt and chuckle. "You were never exactly a handyman, Eli. What happened?"

"Prison," Eli replies simply. "They offered courses, so I took them. Figured that half a year didn't need to be a total waste, plus I needed to keep busy."

He ducks back into the living room and Dad and I exchange an amused look. Eli and I are actually a lot alike.

"See you tonight?" I say as I head for the door.

"You got it."

I pause in the doorway. "And Dad? Thank you."

Dad smiles. "Of course, Bracha."

***

On my lunch break, I walk a few blocks to Cam's Cafe. I sit near the back, prepared to zone out on my phone for the next forty-five minutes. When someone appears next to my table, I mumble a *thanks* and navigate to Dani's feed.

"Thanks for what?"

Startled, I look up to see not the waiter with my sandwich but Maddy.

"Oh!" Blinking, I set my phone face down on the table. "Um, hi."

Maddy pulls out the chair opposite me and sits. "Hi."

"How'd you know I was here?"

"It's Monday. Tuna salad sandwich day. No onion." Maddy smiles smugly as the waiter sets my sandwich down. "Voila."

I try to hide a mixture of amusement and annoyance as I thank the waiter. "Guess I'm as predictable as ever."

"Not really." Maddy picks a carrot off my plate and pops it into her mouth. "You fucked off to Israel for a few months. Very unpredictable."

"True." I pick up my sandwich, then set it down. "Maddy, I really am sorry about—"

I stop when she waves her hand. "We did this on the phone, Bracha. It's fine, really. We're good."

Relieved, I let out a long exhale. "Okay. Good."

"*This* is the reason I wanted to see you." Lightning fast, Maddy swipes up my phone. "I see. Just as I suspected."

She flashes the screen at me and I get a glimpse of

Dani posing on what I'm pretty sure is the Brooklyn Bridge. I attempt to snatch my phone back, but Maddy holds it up like a kid playing Piggy in the Middle.

"Who is she?" Maddy studies the photo. "Pretty cute, I'll give you that. You've been liking every single thing she posts over the last few days. She's in New York but I'm guessing you met her in Tel Aviv?"

"Are you stalking me on Facebook Maddy?" I take a giant bite of my sandwich, trying to look unbothered as Maddy flips through more of Dani's photos.

"Don't dodge the question, Bracha?" Maddy taps on the screen.

"She worked at the hostel I stayed at." I concede.

"And?"

Groaning, Maddy slides my phone across the table. "Bracha, come on. Just tell me."

"Tell you what?" I give her my best mock innocent look. If she's going to act like a kid on the playground, so will I.

"Alright, I'll just say it." Maddy leans back in her chair and crosses her arms. "We meet up one night and out of nowhere, you start talking about wanting to get married and have kids. I foolishly think you're talking about us and then you show me the list you made of all the qualities your perfect wife will have and how you're going to find her. A few days later, you fly halfway around the world."

I take another bite of sandwich and shrug. Maddy arches a perfectly tweezed brow.

"You went to Israel to find a girl. And clearly you did." Reaching out, she taps my phone again. "Only said girl is now in New York. But you're here, moping around with a tuna sandwich."

I glance over at the photo of Dani whilst trying to chew the mouthful of sandwich in my cheek, but I have lost all sense of appetite.

"So why the hell aren't you there Bracha?"

I ignore Maddy's question.

"It's not like you to give up." Maddy pushes again taking another carrot, staring straight at me.

Maddy's smug expression and her look of amusement suddenly makes tears well up in my eyes. I feel so incredibly bare that I force the swallow in my throat and choke with more tears.

Maddy's expression quickly changes to one of alarm.

"Oh, shit, Bracha. I'm sorry, I didn't mean to…"

It's my turn to wave my hand. "No, no, it's fine. Crying is something I do a lot these days, apparently."

Pushing my sandwich aside, I take a deep breath. Then I tell Maddy the entire story, slowly, thoroughly, as if I was talking to my mother, I confide in her about everything. Eli and the house, running away to Israel, the terrible dates, Sol passing away, and then…Dani. She listens intently without passing judgement and without showing her feelings of hurt and anger which I can tell are still there. That is, until I get to the list that Dani made the last time I saw her.

"You absolute idiot," she says when I finish. "That list was about you."

"I know."

"She's into you."

"Maybe."

"Maybe?" Maddy scoffs. "Why *maybe*?"

"Her grandfather had just died," I say, pushing a crumb around my plate. "She was grieving, emotional, you know. I was there, and her girlfriend wasn't. It might've just been that. Besides, she's in New York now, so clearly, she and Riley worked things out."

"Oh yeah, clearly she worked things out with her cheating girlfriend," Maddy says sarcastically, scooping up my phone and swiping again. "That's why she hasn't posted a single thing about her since she got to New York."

I chew my lip. "You think they broke up?"

"I think you're an idiot and avoiding the real issue here." Maddy's thumbs fly over my screen. "The question is, are you going to keep moping around being a loser? Or are you going to go after her?"

She shoves the phone at me. The browser is open to a list of flights from Sydney to New York.

"You can't be serious," I tell her.

"You can't be this thick." Maddy grabs the pickle spear off my plate and wags it at me like a schoolteacher. "You were willing to fly to Tel Aviv to look for literally *any* woman that fits your stupid list criteria for a hypothetical *perfect*. And now you aren't even willing to fly to New York to make things right with the one you actually fell in love with?"

Her last few words take my breath away. Because my heartstrings instantly resonate with the simple clarity, the *truth* behind them.

I am in love with Dani.

I select a flight for this weekend and pull out my wallet. "This is crazy," I tell Maddy, my pulse racing. She takes a bite of pickle and winks at me.

"That's how you know it's love."

Chapter Nineteen

I step onto the NYU campus without a plan. I left Victoria in shock when I got back to work from lunch with Maddy and told her I need another week off work, maybe even longer. But losing my job seems inconsequential when it compares to losing Dani.

Over the last twenty-four hours, I've typed at least a hundred different texts to Dani. Every single one has gone unsent because they were all absurd.

Funny story, I won a trip to New York! Want to meet up?

I just happen to be in the neighbourhood…

Have you found any place that makes a black coffee as good as The Galya? Maybe one near Washington Square Park?

I'm coming to NYC. We need to talk.

I miss you.

I…

The first thing I do is visit the administration building. A middle-aged woman with close-cropped black curls and bright yellow framed glasses greets me with a professional smile.

"I'm here to see a friend," I say, wiping my sweaty palms on my jeans. "I was hoping you could share her schedule with me. Dani Rosenberg?"

Her smile falters ever so slightly. "I'm sorry, I can't share student information. I'm sure if you call or text her, she can let you know where to meet her."

"It's a surprise," I blurt out, my face heating up. "I'm visiting from Australia."

"That's nice," the woman says, but I'm pretty sure I detect a hint of suspicion in her eyes. "I'm sorry. It would be against the rules for me to share a student's schedule. I'm sure you understand."

I do. But that doesn't make it any less frustrating.

I wander the corridors of the building, trying to come up with a plan. None of Dani's posts have revealed anything about her schedule. Now that I'm here and I can see the size of the NYU campus—and Manhattan in general—it's dawning on me that I could spend a month here and not run into her.

Just text her, loser, says a little voice in my head that sounds remarkably like Maddy. I ignore it. After all, if Dani responds that she doesn't want to see me, it's over. Better she sees me, face to face.

I find myself in a corridor lined with various art projects. One catches my eye and my breath comes to a complete stop.

It's a collage that mixes photography and painting and it takes up at least the entire length of the wall. The right side depicts a beach with choppy grey waves painted in familiar brush strokes. My heart resumes beating, I move over to see the list of contributors in tiny print. My gaze falls on her name right away: *Dani Rosenberg.*

Beneath the students' names, it reads: *Professor Behrens, Visual Arts in the 21st Century.*

I race back to the admin desk. "Sorry to bother you again, but can you tell me where and when the Visual Arts in the 21st Century class meets?"

The woman adjusts her yellow-framed glasses.

"Er…"

"I'm a prospective student," I add hastily. "I understand we're allowed to visit a few classes and I'd like to sit in on that one."

I'm taking a gamble—I don't actually know what NYU's policy is in that regard—but it works. After making a copy of my ID, the woman tells me what I need to know and I'm off and running again.

The course is held in The Barney Building, which is a few long blocks down on Stuyvesant Street. And lucky me, the next class starts in forty minutes.

Ten minutes later, gasping for breath, I burst through the double doors and stop in front of the directory. "Room 203," I say out loud, heading for the elevator. I punch the button once, twice, a whole bunch of times, and then I charge down the hall for the stairs.

I fling the door open to room 203 and stand there, panting like a maniac. It's a large studio space, with about a dozen students spread out at different workstations. At the front, a scowling man in glasses stands in front of a massive, old-school blackboard.

"Can I help you?"

"Yes, sorry," I say, struggling to get my breathing under control. I'm scanning the faces of the students and Dani isn't among them. "I was looking for Visual Arts in the 21st Century? I'm sitting in today."

The professor's scowl deepens. "That class begins in twenty minutes. If you don't mind…"

He literally shoos me out of the room.

Face flushed, I lean against the wall. Was it really

just a few weeks ago that I was calling Josh a cliché for racing through the airport to catch Katya before her flight?

"And here I am," I murmur. "Acting like the protagonist in my own rom-com."

I have to admit, it's not the worst feeling in the world.

Ten minutes later, students file out of the studio. The professor follows, casting another glare in my direction. As soon as they're out of sight, I slip inside. My gaze goes to the blackboard and my feet carry me over to it. Without thinking about it, without even fully knowing what I'm about to do, I pick up a piece of chalk and begin to write.

The Ten Point Woman
1. Looks hot in red denim overalls
2. Knows where to get the best coffee in Tel Aviv
3. Comes from a loving family
4. Pursues her passions
5. Is annoyingly illogical at times
6. Faces her fears
7. Makes every place she touches more beautiful
8. Calls me on my bullshit
9. Is more in touch with her emotions than me
10. Is p—

The door closes loudly, startling me. I whirl around and find Dani standing there. Her eyes wide.

A long moment passes in which we just stare at one another.

Slowly, Dani sets her messenger bag down on the

closest workstation. She takes a few tentative steps forward, her eyes flicking from me to the list. I watch as pink colours her cheeks.

"So," she says finally. "Has your master plan brought you to New York?"

I shake my head. "No plan this time. I bought a ticket and…well. Here I am."

"That's new."

"Yeah."

"But you still have a list." Dani nods at the board. "Although this one has ten points. What's the last one supposed to be?"

Swallowing hard, I step in front of the board and finish writing. Then I move away to see her reaction as she reads.

10. Is perfect.

Amusement flashes in her eyes, but she still doesn't smile. At some point, I realise three more students have entered, and they're watching us curiously as they make their way to various workstations. One, a guy with a man bun that makes me miss Josh fiercely, raises his hand.

"Yes?" I say.

He gives me a little smirk. "I think you're in the wrong studio. This is Visual Arts of the 21st Century, not Interpretations of Human Desire."

The other students giggle. Rolling her eyes, Dani grabs my hand and her bag, dragging me out of the studio.

I allow her to pull me down the hallway, enjoying her hand in mind, neither of us speaking a word. Dani

214

shoulders through another door, this one leading to a studio with floor-to-ceiling windows overlooking a courtyard. It's filled with sculptures-in-progress, all of people—an elderly man on a bench feeding pigeons, a young woman in a dress caught mid-twirl, two baby-faced children in the midst of a teddy-bear fight.

"Bracha," Dani says, and I realise her hand is still in mine. "Why are you here? Really?"

"You," I say simply.

Her chest rises and falls, as if she's as out of breath as I am. She looks flustered. "And…and how long are you planning to stay in New York?"

"However long you want me to."

A funny little laugh escapes her lips. "Really?"

"Really." I say more certain than ever.

Dani presses her lips tight before exclaiming, "I ended things with Riley a week before I left Tel Aviv."

I nod seriously, trying to hide my elation. "Why didn't you tell me? Before you left?"

"That would've been far too logical." Now I can tell Dani is trying to suppress a smile.

"Well, I guess it's official then." I say teasing.

"What is?"

"You're the Ten Point Woman."

Dani's cheeks light up.

"So, you actually flew from Sydney to New York to find me? You know, you could've just called. Or texted."

"But…"

"But what?"

"But that would've been far too logical." I pause.

"Love isn't always totally rational. I mean, I know there are logical reasons why I fell in love with you. You're ambitious and funny and smart and you—"

I have to stop because her lips are on mine.

Her kiss makes my whole body warm, like I've stepped into a sunbeam after being lost in a long, dark winter. I slide my free hand gently around her neck, fingers combed in her hair, and she moves closer, pressing herself against me. When we finally pull apart, I feel a complete sense of calm.

"And I what?" she whispers.

"And you make me a little bit crazy."

I kiss her before she can respond, and I can feel her lips smiling against mine.

Epilogue

"We will begin boarding flight QF173 to Sydney in just a few minutes."

Sighing, I glance up from my book and look around the gate. It's going to be a full flight, no doubt about that. I grabbed the last available seats at the gate, squeezed between a rabbi reading the New Yorker and a weary-looking mother with a sleeping infant strapped to her chest.

I try to turn my attention back to my book. It's a paperback I picked up at the airport bookstore—another one of Katya's recommendations—and I'm having a hard time getting into it.

"Try this."

Dani appears in front of me, holding out another book. I squint at the cover and give her a disdainful look.

"How to Stop Overplanning Your Life?"

She nods, stepping back as I stand and finishing her coffee. "Look at the tagline."

I take the book and read the quote along the bottom out loud as we walk away from the seats. *"You can have it all…but do you WANT it all?* Oh, please. This is self-help rubbish at its finest."

We reach the rubbish bin, and Dani tosses her empty coffee cup inside. "It's trash you need, Bracha," she says, planting a loud, smacking kiss on my cheek. "Trust me. Just read the first page."

I play along, flipping the book open. "What's this…"

Two paper tickets fall out. I catch them and turn them over.

"Ben-Gurion?" I stare at Dani in disbelief. "You bought tickets to Tel Aviv? From…" I glance at the tickets again. "Sydney?"

"Sure, looks that way."

"For us?"

Dani laughs. "Who else?"

"But you've only got two weeks off before your first art project is due," I point out, my mind reeling with all the impracticalities. "Factoring in the jet lag from here to Australia, all the activities we planned for Sydney, jet lag *again* from there to Israel, and yet again returning to New York, we won't be able to—"

Dani cuts me off with a kiss, which has proven to be an effective way to shut me up. She bumps her nose against mine briefly, her eyes sparkling.

"Bracha, we can stand here arguing about the logistics, or we can just go for it. Which do you prefer?"

I gaze at Dani, taking in her innocent smile, her tangle of auburn curls piled in a messy bun, the little smudge of blue paint near her temple I noticed at breakfast but still haven't pointed out because I think it's cute. This is what I wanted all along. This crazy, spontaneous yet perfectly understandable kind of love, where every unpredictable moment somehow aligns with reason. My annoyance melts away, replaced with the purest happiness I've felt in a long time.

I take her hand and squeeze.

"I think we'll figure it out together."

***

Dedication

February 14th

How should I describe myself – female, 165 centimetres, brown hair, green eyes – so far so good. Age – now that is relative, relative to my mood, relative to my weight, relative to whether I slept well the night before. Some days I look in my mid to late thirties – others, well let's just say – not in my blooming prime. But today, today I look and feel my age.

It's Valentine's Day and I am at home. Not alone. My 22-year-old daughter is with me. She is encouraging me to register with one of Australia's most successful internet dating services. It's all a little confronting. After my divorce, I was too busy working, raising children, paying bills, doing my doctorate, trying to keep fit and so on and so on – what every thirty-something divorcee is doing these days. Due to the pressures of the noughties, dating has not been a priority, not centre stage, not even in the sidelines.

Let's face it, I have put my love life on hold.

And now, apparently, I'm supposed to condense myself into an online profile. Three hours of effort, minimum. How do you capture the "essential me" in tidy little fields with word limits? All while broadcasting my height, weight, age, and even shoe size for strangers to scroll past.

"Professional, thoughtful, generous individual seeking someone similar" – that's the headline that will attract men from cyberspace.

Then there is this gem: "Divorced, two children (not living at home), don't want any more of my own, but yours are fine." I like that line. It sounds tolerant and accepting — says a lot, if you think about it.

Now for the hardest part – what am I looking for, who is my ideal partner? Now that is hard.

***

These are my mother's words. Her dream was to write a romantic comedy about divorced women in the early 2000s, when internet dating was just beginning to take off and change how people met. She had the courage to put herself out there online.

I, on the other hand, took the pragmatic route: a checklist. Write a list, tick the boxes, get the job done. In the end, that list helped me find the love of my life.

My writing is inspired by my mother's bravery.

And in her memory, I dedicate this book to her.

9 781764 353434

Praise for "The Ten Point Woman"

The Ten Point Woman is a rollicking tale of love, loss and meticulous lists that lead to chaos…This gorgeous debut novel sparkles with wit as well as with probing insights into the mess that our emotional landscapes can be. A joy to read!
— Lee Kofman, author of *The Writer Laid Bare*

The Ten Point Woman reminds us that love defies our best-laid plans. Through Bracha's search for her ideal partner, this novel shows that love isn't bound by lists, logic, or place. Both funny and thought-provoking, The Ten Point Woman is a story about the impossibility of controlling where—or with whom—our hearts ultimately lead us.
— Howard Lovy, author of *Found and Lost: The Jake and Cait Story*

This is a very quirky book that reads like the wind, a delightful and humorous wind, that is.
— Barry Levy, author of *Burning Bright* and *Shades of Exodus*